Contents

To Mum and Dad,
who made me believe I could do anything.

First published in Great Britain in 2010
by Piccadilly Press Ltd,
5 Castle Road, London NW1 8PR
www.piccadillypress.co.uk

Text copyright © T.M. Alexander, 2010

A catalogue record for this book is available from the British Library.

ISBN: 978 1 84812 063 1 (paperback)

1 3 5 7 9 10 8 6 4 2

Printed in the UK by CPI Bookmarque, Croydon, CR0 4TD
Cover design by Patrick Knowles
Cover illustration by Sue Hellard

Goodbye, Copper Pie

the school
summer fair

'Keener, can you believe it?' said Fifty.

I shook my head.

He was staring at Copper Pie, who had just blasted a ball into the top left-hand corner of the goal. We watched Copper Pie get a slap on the back from his partner on the stall, none other than Callum – the meanest and nastiest boy in our class . . . in our year in fact . . . in the whole school probably, maybe even the world, the universe, etc.

'Can you believe he's gone over to the dark side?

I shook my head again. There weren't any words for how I felt.

I looked across for the hundredth time. How could Copper Pie, my oldest friend, be running a stall at the summer fair with *Callum*? Copper Pie was the one who saved me from being bitten by Annabel Ellis in nursery, the one who tickled me to stop me from holding my breath and fainting in the nativity play, the one who ate my lunch every time I didn't like it.

If anyone had told me that he would desert me, desert Tribe, I'd have said they were lying. No way would he ever, ever leave: that's what I would have said. But I was wrong.

I'd been looking forward to the summer fair for ages. We all had, because in Year 6 you're allowed to have your own stall. And of course the five Tribers (me, Fifty, Jonno, Bee and Copper Pie) were doing one together (I'll fill you in on the details later). But at the last minute Copper Pie switched allegiance big time to do 'Save or Score' with Callum.

For a pound you could choose either three shots at Callum in goal or three turns in goal trying to stop Copper Pie scoring. Their sign said, *Save three goals or score three and win a fiver*.

And to make it worse, their stall had the biggest queue. There were masses of dads and toddlers and a few girls and even some mums waiting for a turn. Every time there was a good save or an awesome shot the crowds oooh-ed and aaaaah-ed. Copper Pie was in Man United Away (all black). Callum was in Liverpool Home (red). I wished they weren't the centre of attention. Showing off in front of the rest of Tribe. It didn't seem fair. We, the loyal ones, were doing a stall *together*, the way you should do if you're friends. And we're best friends, better than family.

THE TRIBE FAMILY

FIFTY: Small and likes fire.

BEE: Sleeptalks whole conversations.

KEENER: Is a keener (and surf dude).

COPPER PIE: Football mad, junk food mad, and gets mad about ginger jokes.

JONNO: Looks mad – big Afro and glasses– but isn't. Has moved house and school loads of times, but this time he's staying . . . with Tribe.

If you want to understand how I felt, imagine your mum had left you and chosen another family, a better one, tidier or funnier or better looking. Imagine her having a great time with them, while you stood at the side and watched.

I wanted to bang my head against something hard, except that it would hurt. I wanted to smack Copper Pie in the face and yell, but I've never hit anyone and I didn't want to start with him because he's a lot more experienced with his fists. I turned away and looked back at Fifty. He sighed. We didn't need words to know what the other one was thinking.

Bee and Jonno were sitting cross-legged under our

table, talking to each other. I thought about joining them . . . but I didn't. I stayed where I was and watched all the people enjoying themselves.

There was nothing left on our stall. We ran out twenty-two minutes after the fair started. It didn't matter – we'd made loads of money.

I thought about having a go on 'Splat the Rat'. I'm good at that. If you watch the people who go before you, you can count how many seconds it takes the rat to slide down the pipe. So, when it's your turn, all you have to do is count and, when you reach the magic number, wham the stick at the space below the pipe. Everyone else waits for the rat poke its nose out, but by then it's too late.

I decided not to have a go. I knew it wouldn't make me feel any better. How could it? Tribe couldn't carry on without Copper Pie. I can't explain why. It's not as though he was the leader or anything – we don't have one. But he was part of its beginning and we agreed no one could leave and no one could join. So it was broken. Tribe was broken.

ten days to the summer fair . . . and counting

I'd better start at the beginning.

Ten days before the summer fair we had our first meeting in the new Tribehouse. The Tribers built it in Fifty's garden over the weekend with lots of help from my dad and Copper Pie's dad and no help whatsoever from me because I had tonsillitis. Dad and I had planned to go surfing but I woke up on Saturday with the scratchy throat that always means I'm not going to be able to eat anything but ice cream for a few days. Mum gave me my usual banana-coloured medicine, told Dad the road trip was off and went out shopping with my sisters. She's a doctor so you'd think she'd be sympathetic, but you'd need to be bleeding to death with no pulse for Mum to take any notice.

In a way it was lucky that I was ill because the phone went and we were there to answer it, which we wouldn't have been if we were halfway to the coast with a couple of boards on top of the car.

'Keener. It's me.' It was Copper Pie. 'My dad's mate, the one who said we could have his shed, says it's now or never. Fifty's mum says it's OK to go over. Get your dad too. No one answered at Jonno's. Bee's on her way. It's time to build the —'

I passed the phone to Dad, because talking was like someone sanding my flesh.

'Fine,' he said. 'I'll be right over with my tools.'

Dad spent all weekend over at Fifty's. I sent notes from the living room sofa with design ideas, which they ignored. Good job too, because when I finally saw the Tribehouse there wasn't a single thing I'd have changed. (Except I'd have liked a hammock.) Fifty's dad had even cut a hole in the fence and made a little gate so we can get straight into the garden without going through the house – it's the Tribe cat flap.

At the meeting, all of us, except Fifty, were sitting on the bench. It's the only bit of furniture so far. Fifty was sitting on the safe. (I brought it from home.) It holds all our fact files and the tin for Tribe funds (which is empty except for an I.O.U. that says: *Tribe owes Fifty's mum two hours' hoovering*. It's payment for the see-through plastic she bought for the windows of our hut). There's loads of other stuff too: Bee's rolled-up scroll where she wrote our aims, the Save the Stag poster that we used to make the Head give back our bit of the playground rather than bulldoze it, photos that we're meant to be making into ID cards. Actually . . . it could do with a clear out.

We'd done the fist of friendship so it was time for business.

'Right, you know what we've got to sort out tonight?' said Bee.

'Yes, boss.' Fifty saluted.

'Thank you for that.' Bee did a fake smile. 'It's one week till —'

'Ten days,' I corrected her.

'Thank you for that, Keener!' I got the same smile.

'It's a week . . . and a bit . . . till the summer fair. We've had loads of ideas and done zilch, zero, nothing. So today we need to decide *exactly* what we're doing. Agreed?'

'Yes, Bee,' I said.

'Same,' said Fifty.

'I thought we'd decided,' said Copper Pie. 'Bombs!' He did an evil I'm-going-to-kill-you-all cackle.

'Yes, definitely bombs,' said Jonno. It's funny – when Jonno first came along he seemed to have all the ideas. I don't know if you can pass them on, like head lice, but we're all ideas people now.

'OK, if that's what everyone wants. But it won't take five

of us to sell water bombs.' Bee was in Sergeant-Major mode.

'Too right, said Copper Pie. 'They'll sell themselves.'

'Drench your favourite teacher for 50p,' said Fifty.

'Is that how much we're charging?' I asked. I started to calculate how much money our stall was going to make.

'How much do they cost?' asked Bee.

I'd already found the best price on the internet. 'You can get a thousand water bombs for £14.50 including delivery.'

'Wow! A thousand serious soakings of seriously sad members of staff,' said Fifty. 'An excellent afternoon's fun.'

'How much does one cost then?' asked Copper Pie.

'Work it out, idiot,' said Bee, which was a bit cruel because Copper Pie doesn't even do adding, so dividing . . .

'They're 1.45p each,' I said.

I ignored the rolling eyes. *What's the point of calling me Keener if I don't have all the answers?*

'We can't charge 50p then, can we?' said Bee.

I didn't see why not but I waited to find out.

'We can. We can charge what we like,' said Fifty. 'What matters is how much people will pay for them, not what they cost.'

'I don't think that's fair,' said Bee. 'We should charge enough to make some money, but not squillions.'

Jonno nodded. Shame. I wanted to side with Fifty – a thousand balloons at 50p each would be £500! But Bee and Jonno were probably right. It wouldn't be Tribish to fleece all the other kids we're at school with. We like to get along with everyone . . . well, almost everyone. It's part of what we agreed when we formed Tribe.

BEING TRIBISH MEANS:

- Being fair, not fleecing.
- Looking after the world, not throwing rubbish in the street.
- Not being mean, except to seriously nasty people like Callum and Jamie.
- Liking our horrid patch in the playground, even though it smells.
- Liking Copper Pie, even though he smells (it's his diet, according to Bee).
- Doing the right thing if we can work out what the right thing is.
- Being loyal to each other.
- Only lying if it's really necessary (or really funny).
- Not lighting random fires (only applies to Fifty).

'All right, how about 10p each?' said Fifty.

'And three for 25p,' added Bee, in her new role as Financial Director of Tribe Water Bombs Limited.

'Whatever,' said Copper Pie. 'I'm gunning for Miss Walsh. I'll track her until she's in a crowd and then chuck one over the top. *Smack*, straight on her head.'

'That'll make you popular,' said Bee. (Copper Pie's not what you'd call one of our teacher's *favourites*.)

'I'll be undercover.' He thinks he's some sort of spy, but he's actually a redheaded football hooligan.

'So what else are we going to sell? We've got a whole table,' Bee asked. We all looked at each other. Bee looked at us. 'No ideas? That's good. Because *I've* come up with something.'

'What a surprise!' said Fifty. 'Bee in charge.'

She swung her head so that her black fringe flew in the air, letting Fifty see the mean look she was giving him.

'Bring and Buy.'

'Isn't that what the W.I. do?' I said. 'Bring jam and buy more jam.'

'What's the double you eye?' said Copper Pie.

'It's that glasses shop on the telly. Buy one pair get a second free,' said Fifty, winking.

'Soooo not funny. It's the Women's Institute,' said Bee. 'And who cares who else does it? If it's a good idea, it's a good idea. Full stop.'

'Comma,' said Fifty.

'Exclamation mark,' said Jonno.

WHAT'S THE W.I.?
Watch it!
Warm ice
Wicked idea
What if?
West Indies
Way in
Wrought iron
White ink
Welly it

'Semi-colon,' I joined in.

'Can't we have a proper talk without making up silly lists? We're not in Reception any more.'

'Remember the water tray,' said Fifty. 'I liked the blue sailing boat.'

'Cut!' Bee sliced the air with her hand like one of those karate fighters who leap in the air and shout 'Nee haa'. 'It's only half Bring and Buy really, because instead of people bringing something for the stall and then buying something in exchange, my idea is we forget the money bit and just do swaps. That's really green. Bring what you don't want and take something you do want. It's perfect.'

'But the summer fair's all about money,' said Fifty.

'Says who?' said Bee.

'Well . . . why else have one?'

'If it was only about money, the Head could send round a collecting tin. The fair's meant to be fun. And because it's run by the kids it's meant to show the parents and the grannies what a brilliant school we are.'

'I like it,' said Jonno.

'What? School?' said Copper Pie.

'No, Bring and Buy. I like it.'

'Good,' said Bee. 'So, you lot can do the water bombs and I'll sort out the swap stall.'

'I'll help you, Bee,' said Jonno.

'Weirdo,' said Copper Pie. 'Water bombs or the W.I. and you choose —'

13

'He chooses to save the planet,' said Bee, with a smug smile.

'We'll need loads of stuff to swap,' said Jonno.

'Why don't you get the rest of the school to donate things?' I said.

Bee groaned. 'Keep up, Keener. That wouldn't work. If they give their stuff to us they won't have anything left to "bring" on the day of the fair to swap for a "buy".'

Good point. I decided to leave it to them.

Bee's plan was to go round all the houses on her estate with a wheelbarrow and collect old books and toys and jugs and garden gnomes. Jonno said he'd do the same, but that DVDs might be more popular than creepy miniature men with long white hair, Noddy hats and fishing rods. Fifty thought remote controls that don't work anymore would be good because his baby sister, Probably Rose, likes to chew them.

'We don't want rubbish,' said Bee.

'Yes we do,' said Fifty. 'Anything that doesn't get swapped can go on a massive bonfire afterwards.' (Told you: Fifty and fires!)

'No way, we'll take it to the charity shop. We need to recycle, not add a great cloud of smoke to the air we breathe.'

'But I do love a fire. Couldn't we have a tiny, hardly-even-hot one?'

'Someone sit on him,' said Bee. Copper Pie did. Fifty

squealed like a piglet. Jonno took no notice – he was really keen on Bee's idea.

'We'll have to make sure all the kids at school know to bring things on the day to swap,' he said. 'If not they'll only bring money.'

'Posters,' said Bee. 'We'll ask the Head. And maybe an announcement in assembly. She's bound to agree if I explain what a good use of resources it is. I've just thought – if it works, the school could do a swap stall for Earth Day.' (Bee's meant to be suggesting something for next year's Earth Day, when we've all gone to senior school.)

So the summer fair was all agreed. We handed in our Tribe subs, had a chat about what to buy for the hut (not a lot because we only had £3.78) and then it was time for Fifty to have his tea so we all dived through the cat flap and went home. I walked with Copper Pie for a bit. His plan was to buy all the water bombs himself and co-ordinate an attack on a series of key targets, including his little brother, Charlie.

If only he'd stuck to his plan.

nine days to go and
no definite plans yet

The next day I was running across the playground to catch up with the other Tribers when I was ambushed by Flo – the little sister with the not-so-little voice.

'Keener, what are you going to do at the fair?'

'It's a secret.'

'That's not nice, I'm your sister.'

'You're not nice,' I said.

'I'll tell Mum,' she said.

'You don't have to,' I said. 'She already knows you're not nice.'

I should have been ready for it, but I was busy thinking about all the things we needed to do before the big day. She got me on the left shin with her sparkly purple trainers.

'I'll find out what it is. And I'll tell everyone not to have a go on your stall because you're mean.'

And then the right shin. *Ow!*

'All right, all right,' I said. I didn't want anyone to catch me being pulped by a Year 3. 'I'll tell you.' I leant down to whisper in her ear. 'We're selling home-made chocolate babies.' Flo *loves* babies. She smiled, a rare and frightening sight.

'I want one for free.'

'Fine,' I said. 'Just don't tell anyone. We don't want loads of stalls selling home-made chocolate babies.'

When I made it to our patch under the trees – the home we share with stag beetles, longhorn beetles and other weevils all identified by our resident entomologist, Jonno – I found Bee in tears.

'What's up?'

'Shall I tell the terrible tale?' said Fifty.

Bee nodded.

'Bee's dad has left home.'

Crikey. I searched my stupid head for something to say but all the words were hiding in the creases of my brain. I don't know anyone who's divorced, except Fifty's Uncle Terry.

THE NOT-SO-SAD TALE
OF FIFTY'S UNCLE TERRY

Fifty's Uncle Terry left his wife and ran off with a lady he met at church, to work with poor people somewhere in Africa. One day he cut off all the fingers on one hand with a chainsaw and drove himself to the hospital because he didn't want to upset his new lady. Soon after that they came back to England to visit a plastic surgeon and we all went round for tea to see the hand with only a thumb.

After tea Bee said, 'We hope you get better,' and Fifty's mum said, 'There's no need to worry about Terry. He's "found himself" in Africa.' (She meant he was happy.) And Copper Pie said, 'Pity he couldn't find some fingers'. There was complete silence and red faces from everyone until Uncle Terry slapped his hand of four stumps and a thumb down on his leg and laughed till his tears rolled down his face and along his moustache.

'But he'll be back,' said Copper Pie.

'It's just a question of when,' said Jonno.

So, not divorce, I thought. *Something more complicated.*

'He says he's not coming back until the twins find somewhere else to squat.' Bee sniffed between every word.

Now I understood. The twins have jobs and a car and are really old. Bee's mum likes having 'her boys' at home but Bee's dad keeps trying to chuck them out. He'd obviously given up and moved out instead.

'Do you know where he is?' said Jonno.

Bee shook her head. 'They had a row and then he went to football and didn't come back.'

Copper Pie made a strange noise and wriggled.

'What it is?' said Fifty. 'Are you trying to burp?'

'He's at mine. I think. Bee's dad. Maybe. At mine. Maybe.' It came out of C.P. like a volley of bullets.

'What?!' shouted Bee. 'Why didn't you tell me right away?'

Copper Pie looked worried. More worried than when he was sent to the Head for throttling Jonno (before Jonno was a mate).

'Don't kill me.'

Bee didn't – she was too busy crying.

'Is he at yours or not, Copper Pie?' I asked. It seemed as though someone should. There were too many 'maybes'.

'Yes, but I didn't know it until Bee said she didn't know where he was.'

'You aren't making any sense, Copper Pie,' said Jonno. 'Have you seen Bee's dad?'

'No.'

'So why did you say you had?' I asked.

'Because I saw his trainers.'

'But no body,' said Fifty.

'No. If there was a body I'd have known it was Bee's dad.'

It wasn't the most straightforward of conversations.

'We're not following you,' said Jonno.

'There were two big trainers at the top of the stairs when I left for school. And when I was in bed last night

19

I heard Mum and Dad laughing so I reckoned there was someone —'

'Laughing?' Bee hunched her shoulders and stared down at the floor.

Jonno nudged Copper Pie who caught on pretty quickly . . . for him anyway.

'Maybe not laughing. No. More like crying.'

I winked at him. You could tell he felt uncomfortable about harbouring the criminal at his house, even if he'd only just realised.

'Why would Bee's dad go to yours?' asked Jonno. I forget that he doesn't know everything about us. He's only been here a few weeks but the rest of us have been friends forever.

Bee's dad and Copper Pie's dad play football together on Wednesdays and Sundays. It's a team for old people and Copper Pie says they're Rubbish with a capital R. He also says that on Wednesdays, the football's in the pub. It made sense that Bee's dad had gone to a mate's. That's what I'd do if I ran away. I'd go to Jonno's because he's got a fantastic bedroom with loads of techy stuff and his mum and dad are cool and he's got no brothers or sisters to mess things up.

'Come home with me after school,' said Copper Pie. 'We'll see if he's still there.'

'No, thanks,' said Bee. 'If he doesn't want to live with us, you can have him.'

Oh dear!

I really wanted to get on with the water bomb discussions. Should I ask Dad to order them? Should I make a sign for the stall? Who was making posters? What should we put the money in? But something told me we were meant to carry on with the sorry-your-Dad's-gone discussion so I shut up and let Jonno and Fifty try and make things better.

Jonno asked Bee why her dad didn't want to live with her brothers. She told him about all the things they DIDN'T do: wash up, wash their hands, wash their feet, change their socks, clean their teeth, cook, put the toilet seat back down, change the sheets, go to the supermarket, turn the telly off, clear away after tea.

And then she told him all the things they DID do: eat everything in the fridge even if it says *Don't Eat*, watch telly till three o'clock in the morning *on loud*, bring friends home without asking, borrow Dad's stuff and lose it, sleep in till lunchtime, borrow money from Mum (Dad won't lend them any) and *never* pay it back. Eat even more. Stay in bed even later. Watch more telly.

'Sorry, Bee, but it sounds to me like your Dad's right,' said Fifty. 'I mean, they are nineteen —'

'Twenty.'

'That's ancient,' said Fifty. 'I'm not going to live with my mum when I'm twenty.'

'I'd rather not live with mine now,' said Copper Pie.

'I'm pretty sure she feels the same about you,' said

Bee. She sounded a bit more like herself – insulting – so I thought I'd say what I thought.

'Maybe the twins should move out?'

She sighed and put her hands on her hips.

'Of course they should move out, Keener. Everyone knows that . . . well, except Mum. But everyone knows dads aren't meant to run away from their kids either. It's kids that are meant to run away, not parents.'

I'd said the wrong thing, clearly.

only eight
days left

As we hadn't had a chance for a proper talk I made a list of everything we had to do for the stall. Some things were quite urgent – like ordering the water bombs. I needed a Tribe decision.

I met Fifty on the corner, as usual, to walk to school. Mum takes Flo in the car but I never have a lift even if it's raining. Walking's better.

'Guess what?' said Fifty.

Guesswhats are always to do with Probably Rose. I didn't really want to guess but he gets stressy if you don't pretend to be as excited as he is about his baby sister.

'Probably Rose can do a roly-poly?'

'No. Be serious.'

'OK. Well, we know she can say "yoghurt", so my guess is she's learnt another word.' If every word Probably Rose said was going to have its own story, conversations with Fifty were going to get *very* dull.

'Exactly right, my clever friend. Do you want to know what it is?'

'Of course,' I said. *Of course not*, I thought.

'Star.' Fifty looked at me with a beaming smile.

'Great,' I said.

'She looked up at the light and just said it.' I didn't bother pointing out that a star is not the same as a light bulb. Copper Pie and Jonno were by the school gate, but no Bee.

'*Is* Bee's dad at yours?' Fifty asked Copper Pie.

He nodded. 'I didn't see him last night but the trainers were there again this morning.'

'You must know who's staying with you. Didn't you eat dinner with him? Didn't your mum say you had a guest?' said Jonno, a bit puzzled.

Copper Pie didn't answer so I helped out. 'He eats tea with the nursery kids.'

And so did Fifty. 'And his mum isn't that chatty. She tends to work on a need-to-know basis.'

'Not all parents are quite like yours, Jonno,' I said. I don't think he realised dinner with place settings and proper food only went on at his.

'Copper Pie, are you sure they're Bee's dad's trainers?' I asked. Footwear didn't seem to be the most reliable way of identifying someone.

'Good point, Keener,' Fifty said. 'Did you look for a name, Copper Pie?'

I laughed and so did Jonno, but Copper Pie didn't join in.

'The shoes weren't named. I looked underneath and inside.'

'Grown-ups don't have labels. Divvy!' said Fifty. 'Unless . . . does your mum label you, Copper Pie?'

Fifty grabbed C.P.'s arms and turned them over looking for a label. He tried to look down the back of his T-shirt but he wasn't tall enough to see so I did.

'There it is,' I shouted. I pretended to read the label. 'A ginger nut with fast legs and a permanently empty stomach. Feed several pork pies daily, wash once a month and dry flat.'

Copper Pie pushed me away and ran round to the Tribe patch, also known as the scrubby, damp, dark bit between the netball courts and the tree. We followed, laughing because Fifty'd pretended to spot C.P.'s barcode.

As Bee wasn't there it seemed a good time to get on with the list. (We didn't need her anyway because she was swap stall.) I got it out but . . .

'I rang Bee last night,' said Fifty. 'She said her mum says her dad can't come back ever.'

'Why not?' said Jonno.

'I'm not sure,' said Fifty. 'Bee wasn't making much sense.'

'Is she coming to school?' asked Copper Pie.

Fifty nodded. But she didn't come. So at lunch I finally got to go through the list.

WATER BOMBS STALL

Decide where to order the bombs from – Tribe
Order the water bombs – Keener
Pay for them somehow? – Ask Keener's dad to
      use his card
Make a sign for the stall – Tribe
Ask Flo if we can borrow her shop till – Keener
Get something to put the water bombs in?

It all seemed straightforward until Copper Pie said, 'How are we gonna fill the balloons?'

I looked at Fifty and said, 'How *are* we going to fill the balloons?'

Fifty looked at Jonno. 'How —?'

'I don't know,' said Jonno.

Copper Pie made a smug face. Fair enough. It's not often he spots something we've all missed.

If you've never filled a water bomb, you've obviously been living in Darkest Peru like that marmalade bear, but I'll tell you anyway. It's not that easy. You have to stretch the top of the mini-balloon over the tap and make it full enough to be round but not so full that you can't tie the knot. Filling a thousand water bombs was not going to be a small job.

'We can't do it on the day,' said Fifty. 'No tap. Not enough time.'

'Well we'll have to do it at home . . . I suppose,' I said.

More problems were occurring to me. A thousand full-to-bursting water bombs would be heavy and take up a lot of room.

'Could we do it at school?' said Fifty.

'We could . . . but where? The water fountain's no good and I don't fancy doing it in the loo.' I made a face designed to mimic the idea of spending an hour in the not-that-clean bogs.

'We could use the art room – that's got a tap. Let's ask Mr Morris,' said Jonno.

Mr Morris likes us because Jonno showed him the stag beetle that lives under the trees where we hang out.

'Off you go then, Jonno,' said Fifty.

'OK.'

Jonno went, leaving us to discuss targets. Top of the list were: Callum (number one enemy of Tribe), Jamie (Callum's shadow), Miss Walsh and Flo (she got my vote).

'Somebody absolutely *has* to bomb the Head,' said Fifty.

Well, it won't be me, I thought. I'd get caught (or miss completely more like). As usual, Copper Pie thought differently. 'Sounds like a job for me. I could use my catapult to lob the bomb. More speed, better aim *and* I could be further away – less chance of getting caught.'

I could see there was going to be trouble at the fair.

'Do you think we should go over to Bee's after school?' said Fifty.

'I can't,' I said. I could, but I didn't want to. I'm no good at the soppy stuff. I mean, what do I know about dads leaving home?

'Me neither,' said Copper Pie.

'Looks like it's only me then,' said Fifty.

'Let us know what's going on,' said Copper Pie.

I wasn't that bothered. It's not like her mum and dad were splitting up. It seemed simple to me. Patrick and the other twin (I can't remember his name. I've only seen him about twice, and even then he might have been the other one as they both look the same) should move out and it would be fine again. Better, in fact, because of all the things Bee said about washing and money and telly.

At home I got on with buying the water bombs. I found a better site, selling a hundred for 99p. Billy bargain! All I needed was credit card details so I got Dad. He finishes early on Friday.

'What's this about then?'

He never knows what's going on. One of us could leave home and he wouldn't notice for a week. He's always away somewhere doing something that nobody knows about (or wants to). I don't mind because when he is here he hangs round with me, which Mum never does. Our family is sort of divided. Mum and Amy (my big sister) and Flo (my little sister) go and watch girly films and Dad and I watch action movies. They go shopping and we go off for the day, surfing (or skimboarding if there's no swell). It's great because there's a long car journey – we listen to music, eat snacks we buy from the garage, and chat – and then we get changed into our wet-suits, and we stay in the sea till we're blue and can't grip the leash. Then it's time for hot grub at the café on the beach and a hot chocolate. I fall asleep on the way home *every* time.

Dad's asked me loads of times if I want to take someone but I like being with him on my own, although I might invite Jonno one day. Fifty's too puny and Copper Pie can't swim very well and Bee's a girl . . .

'Dad, what's going on is that we're having a stall at the fair.'

'Great. You haven't done that before, have you?'

'You're only allowed one in Year 6.'

'That explains it,' said Dad with a wink. 'And what's yours?'

'Water bombs.'

'Guaranteed to sell out,' he said. 'Top idea.'

'And a "Bring and Buy".'

'Like the W. I.?'

I explained Bee's swap stall.

'All sounds good to me. Except it's not really "Bring and Buy" if you don't buy. It's more like "Give and Take".'

'Whatever. But I need *you* to do some buying.'

Dad tapped in all his card details and asked for next-day delivery, which isn't actually next day.

'If you order before twelve noon you get the parcel the next day but after that it becomes the day after the next day.'

'Shouldn't it be called day-after-tomorrow delivery then?' I asked.

'I can't be bothered to answer that,' said Dad.

He always says that when I make a picky point. He says I'm pedantic. I thought that meant I had feet with toes, which I do, but it doesn't. It means I like things to be correct.

We all went out for supper, and Amy's spotty boyfriend came too. I didn't say anything to him. He talked to Dad about rugby, which I hate. I told Mum about Bee's dad. She looked really shocked and said I should have told her before, so she could ring and see how things were. I was starting to get the idea that perhaps it was more serious than I thought.

a week
to go

THE BREAKFAST MENU

KEENER: Crispy bacon in two slices of crusty white bread in front of the computer.

AMY: Wholemeal bread, spread with Marmite, dipped in egg and fried. On a tray because teenagers can't get up!

FLO: Fried egg and potato waffles in front of the telly.

MUM: A pot of tea in bed.

DAD: Fried egg, bacon, beans and toast, reading the paper.

Saturday mornings are good. Dad does the breakfast. It takes ages and we all get different food at different times delivered to different places. We stay in pyjamas until he suddenly realises we're going to be late and then there's a mad rush to get ready for swimming (me) and ballet (Flo). Amy and Mum have a lie-in.

On the way to the pool I texted Copper Pie to see if he wanted to meet up later in the park.

The reply said: *COME OVERHEER.*

I hadn't been to his for a while. He'd rather come to mine and I'd rather *not* go to his. His mum shouts at him. And doesn't talk to me, unless I'm in the way.

Copper Pie was kicking a ball against his garage door. It was so loud I could hear it before I turned into his street. I joined in.

'I've got to look after Charlie. Mum's going to the supermarket,' he said. *I* wouldn't leave Charlie with him. He's hardly babysitter material.

'In here, you two!' Copper Pie's mum shouted from the kitchen. We went straight in. Some people have to be obeyed.

'Charlie's having his nap. I need you to stay *in* the house while I do the shopping and when I come back you can have a bag of crisps each. If he wakes up, go and get him and *be nice* until I get back. If Dad gets back before I do you can go to the park. Understood?'

I nodded.

'Yes, Mum.'

She was gone. See, she doesn't bother with 'Hello, how are you?' It's all instructions.

'Where's your dad then?'

'Gone out with Bee's dad.'

'So you've seen Bee's dad then?'

'Nope. I didn't see any dads last night, or trainers, but this morning Mum said Dad had gone off early to watch a game over in Tyndall with a *mate* – so it must be Bee's dad.' Copper Pie paused and made a moody face. 'He usually watches me play.'

'What shall we do?' I said. We used to say that all the time. No one ever had a good idea. Jonno changed all that. Or maybe Tribe did.

'We could get the guns out. Aim from my window and —'

'Yet me out!' It was Charlie's voice, coming through the baby monitor. He's three, not really a baby. He can talk quite well, except he can't say Ls, Rs or THs. They're either Ys, Ws or Vs.

'Yet me out!'

'We'd better go,' I said.

'No way. Leave him.'

'Yet me out, Mum!'

'We can't leave him, he'll —'

'He'll what?' said Copper Pie.

'He'll be upset.'

33

'All right, Softy. You can get him if you like.'

'Mum! Yet me out!'

I didn't really want to, but I didn't want C.P.'s mum to come home and find him screaming either.

'Back in a minute,' I said. The hall of their house is spotless. No shoes, no brollies, not even anything on the bottom step waiting to be taken upstairs. It's because they run a nursery and there are rules about being tidy and clean. We're not allowed in any of the rooms on the ground floor, except the kitchen. Even at the weekend when there aren't any little kids there, we still can't go in. Everything, apart from cooking and eating, goes on upstairs in their house. The staircase goes round a corner to get to the first floor and *that's* when it all changes. I stepped over dirty washing, two books, the sucky bit from the hoover, a fluffy scarf, a toothbrush, a yoyo, a shin pad and a bowl with the remains of an apple in it (or possibly banana), and that was only what was on the first lot of stairs. The second set was just as bad.

At the top I turned first right into Charlie's bedroom. He was lying under his duvet cuddling a square of grey blanket. As soon as I stepped on his carpet he put it under his pillow and got up. Charlie *never* gets out of bed unless someone comes to get him, because his mum says he mustn't. It's not normal to be so obedient. He's the opposite of his brother!

'Hi Charlie,' I said.

'Heyyo Keener.' It's hard not to laugh about the 'l' thing. (Copper Pie makes him say lollipop - yoyyipop.) I think his nappy was full but I wasn't going to mention it. He waddled off, through all the debris. I followed him back down the stairs all the way to the kitchen.

'Heyyo.'

'Hello Snot,' said Copper Pie.

Charlie smiled. I don't think he knows it's an insult.

'Can we make a marble wun?'

'Make it yourself, Snot.'

'I'll do it with you,' I said. We got the box out from the kitchen cupboard. I'm a whizz at marble runs. I heard feet on the stairs and then the noise of the telly coming on in the room above. Copper Pie had deserted me. Charlie chose a clear marble with a green swirl.

'Weady.'

'Hang on,' I said. 'I haven't made it yet.' Charlie watched me construct a few towers and link them together.

The back door banged open and in walked Copper Pie's dad and another man – a stranger who definitely wasn't Bee's dad. I looked at his feet. Big white trainers.

'There's my Charlie-boy.'

'I'm pwaying wiv Keener.'

'Where's your big brother?'

'He's in the telly room,' I said.

'Get down here and turn the googlebox off,' shouted Copper Pie's dad. (Everyone shouts in their house.) More feet-on-the-stairs noise.

'This is my son.' He pointed to Copper Pie who had

appeared in the doorway. 'And this is my old friend Simon.'
He put his arm round the stranger. I didn't care who he was.
I was more interested in the mystery of where Bee's dad had
been since Wednesday if he hadn't been at C.P.'s. Maybe
he'd fallen over and knocked himself out and was wandering
around the streets with no idea what his name was . . . like
that piano man. Maybe he'd be in the newspaper, *Bee's dad
found with no memory except every Man United football score
ever.*

THE TRUE STORY OF PIANO MAN
BY KEENER

A man was found wandering with no identification on
him. He couldn't speak. He was handed over to the
police because no one knew what to do with him.
They gave him some paper so he could write his name
and address but all he did was draw a picture of a
grand piano. They found him one and he sat down
and played like a professional.

No one knew where he lived or what had
happened to him to make him not be able to speak. All
they ever knew was that he was a fantastic pianist.

'Pleased to meet you. I hear you're football crazy,' said
the stranger.

Copper Pie grunted. He's rubbish at talking to adults.

'Simon and me used to play football together when we

were kids. How many windows d'you think we broke?' said C.P.'s dad.

'Too many to count,' said Simon the stranger, and they both laughed. I don't get that about grown-ups. If Copper Pie broke a window he'd be for it, but they broke loads, and for some reason it's funny.

Copper Pie's dad smiled a big smile and said, 'Simon is a scout. A real scout.'

Big deal! I pictured him dressed in a green scout shirt with a red necker, wearing his huge trainers, and tying silly knots with his fat fingers.

'Keener! A scout!'

Copper Pie started bouncing, like a puppy. I couldn't imagine why. Charlie clapped but there was no way he understood either.

'Great,' I said. I didn't want to burst his bubble. Maybe he fancied joining.

'He's working for one of the big clubs. He can't say who.' Copper Pie's dad winked at Simon. 'It's all hush-hush. They're interested in a player from round here.'

I'd caught up. We were talking football. A football scout, not the sort you find at a jamboree. No wonder Copper Pie was excited.

'I'm going back up north later on today but I'm coming back to watch a game next Saturday. Your dad says you're a handy player, and a left-footer, I understand. A good left-footer is gold dust. Might see you in action one day?'

I thought my redheaded friend was going to collapse.

'Breathe, Copper Pie.' It was the first time I'd had to tell someone else to breathe. It was always me who forgot to inhale and ended up on the floor.

'I'll put the kettle on,' said Copper Pie's dad. 'Get lost, you lot. We've got things to talk about.'

'This could be my big break, Keener,' whispered Copper Pie, as we walked out. I was pleased for him, of course, but football's not my thing so I muttered a bit and nodded and eventually we went out the back and catapulted stones at a can on the bird table. Charlie came too. He collected up the stones and brought them back to us.

'Shall we go to the park then?' I said. It was boring in the garden.

'No way. I'm staying here. He's a scout, Keener! He could discover me. Make me the youngest ever player in the Premiership. He could be scouting for Man United! I could end up playing in the black strip for real.'

six days
till D-day

Sundays are 'family day' in our house. We have Sunday lunch. The kids peel all the vegetables, lay the table and get the drinks to help Mum. Afterwards we're all meant to do something nice together, like a walk or a bike ride. Sundays are boring. So I asked Fifty to come over and didn't tell Mum. I knew she wouldn't tell him to get lost. We're not like that.

'Hello there, you're just in time for lunch. Would you like to stay?'

'Oh! Yes please,' said Fifty, acting surprised. 'Your Sunday lunch is much better than ours.' Fifty's mum tries to be a proper mum, but she's not that good on the cooking front.

'I'd better give your mum a call.'

'No need. She already —' Fifty's sentence finished in mid-air. Mum waited but nothing happened.

'Well, we'd better lay another place,' she said, glancing at the table where . . . *Oops!* I'd already laid six. *That wasn't bright.* She gave me a suspicious look. 'You must be telepathic. Either that or bad at counting.'

'Come on.' We legged it.

I told Fifty about Copper Pie's almost famous guest. He was gobsmacked.

He told me about Bee's dad. *I* was gobsmacked.

'He came home on Friday night. No one knows where he'd been. I was still at Bee's. Her mum had made a huge bowl of tuna pasta with beans. It was awesome. I was hurrying to make sure I got seconds when he walked in. She said, "So you've come back".' Fifty stood with his hands on his hips pretending to be a cross wife. 'And he said, "It's my home, isn't it?" and she said, "Not if you're not prepared to share it with your kids".'

'Did they have a fight?' My parents don't row in front of us. They do it when we're in bed.

'Almost. She shoved him out of the door and locked it.'

'What did you do?'

'I carried on eating.'

'What about Bee?'

'She said it served him right for trying to blackmail the family.'

'Wasn't she upset?'

'Not really – she's on her mum's side. We finished tea and then she dragged me round the estate collecting for the swap stall.'

'Did you get much?'

'Loads. But no remote controls.'

'What about garden gnomes?'

'No. But we got some crutches, and a loudspeaker.'

'Cool,' I said. 'And I ordered the water bombs.'

'How many?'

'A thousand.'

'Oh yes! A thousand bombings. The Head'll never ever let anyone have a water bomb stall ever again. What does she think everyone's going to do with them? Water the grass?'

Flo arrived at the door of my room.

'Lunch is ready. Who's watering the grass?'

'No one, Flo,' I said.

'It's to do with the fair,' said Fifty.

'You're doing chocolate babies. Keener told me.'

'Chocolate babies?' Fifty said, laughing. 'In your dreams, Flo.'

She ran back downstairs. As we walked into the kitchen I heard, 'But Keener lied to me, Mummy. He said I could have a free chocolate baby.'

I would have got a telling off except . . . surprise, surprise . . . there was yet another place laid and spotty boyfriend was sitting at it. No way was Mum going to lay into me in front of him. All she said was, 'It's not nice to eat babies. Chocolates should really only be chocolate-shape.'

Chocolate doesn't have a shape but I didn't bother to point that out.

* * *

After lunch Fifty wanted to go and see the others. In theory I have to stay home but we rang Jonno from my mobile and got him to ring back on the house phone and invite me over to help him with signs for the stall. An excellent idea – it was Fifty's.

'Just this once then,' said Mum. 'Although I was looking forward to a family walk to work off the lunch.' She patted her tummy.

We rang Bee and Copper Pie on the way. Copper Pie said he was busy! Unheard of. Bee said she'd meet us at Jonno's.

'Where are we going then?' said Jonno. He was standing outside his house.

'We were coming to yours,' said Fifty. 'That's why we're here.' As if to show he really was there he pointed at his shoes. I've never really looked at them before. They're tiny. But I suppose big feet would be odd when he's so small.

'You said we could make signs,' I said.

'That's what *you* told me to say. You can't make signs at my house. That would mean paint and mess – things Mum and Dad hate.'

I was disappointed. Jonno's house is the best.

'Let's go to the Tribehouse then,' said Fifty.

We went through the cat flap. I was last and by the time I got into the garden the Tribers had frozen, like musical statues when the music has stopped. Bee pressed her finger against her lips. 'Shhhushhh . . .'

'We've heard feet,' whispered Fifty. 'Moving about.'

I had lots of questions. Soft feet like rabbits' paws? Clackety feet like horseshoes? Clogs? Scratchy feet with claws? But all I said was, 'Where?'

'Shhhushhh . . .'

'There's someone in there,' mouthed Fifty.

I reckoned they were playing a trick on me. I took a step towards the shed but Jonno shook his head. I took a step back. Fifty signalled for us to follow him up to the house. I was getting the idea there really might be a person – a dangerous person.

'Who is it?' I said.

'Shhhushhh . . .' said Fifty. 'We don't know, do we? But he might be dangerous.'

An escaped prisoner loose in the Tribehouse. He could be armed. I ran up the garden to the back door, leaving the others behind. Look out for yourself, I say. Not very Tribish, but being a hero's not my thing.

Fifty's mum was in the kitchen, singing 'Dancing Queen' really loudly. We all spoke at once. She didn't hear a word we said. Fifty pressed 'Off' on the remote control. We all spoke at once again.

'Calm down, Tribers. One at a time,' she said.

So Bee did the talking – how unusual!

'There's someone in the Tribehouse. Someone who shouldn't be there. He sounds . . . big. Maybe dangerous even.'

'Probably dangerous,' said Fifty.

I nodded.

'What a lot of fuss you're making about probably nothing. It's most likely a homeless person. You stay here and I'll go and see. He won't want a whole Tribe staring at him.' That was so typical of Fifty's mum. My mum would have called the police, or my dad at least, but Fifty's mum is the sort who'll invite anyone in. She disappeared down the garden.

We waited. We waited for really quite a long time. I was starting to worry about her. Maybe . . .

'Maybe he's a murderer. Mum wouldn't stand a chance,' said Fifty. He looked like he might cry.

One of us should do something, I thought. Then I changed my thought to: *One of the others should do something.* I looked at Jonno – surely he would announce a plan to storm the Tribehouse and rescue Fifty's mum. Shame Copper Pie wasn't with us – we could have sent him.

At last, voices! They were coming up the path to the house. The tramp had obviously been invited in, as predicted.

'Dad! What are you doing here?' shouted Bee.

Curiouser and curiouser. The *tramp* was Bee's dad. I don't know who was most embarrassed – Bee, who was hiding behind her long black fringe, or her dad, who was stuck to the doormat looking like he might reverse straight back out.

'Why don't you go back to the Tribehouse while we have a chat?' said Fifty's mum.

Fine by us. Me, Fifty and Jonno made it out but . . .

'Not you, Bee. I think your dad has something he'd like to say to you.'

Back in the Tribehouse, Fifty sat on the safe – his favourite spot.

'Where do you think he's been since Wednesday?' said Jonno.

'Maybe he's been here all the time?' said Fifty.

'It'll all be fine now anyway,' I said.

They both made a how-do-*you*-know? face.

'Fifty, your mum earns a living sorting people out, doesn't she?

He nodded.

'So, she'll sort out Bee's family. That's what she *does*.'

And of course she did. When we went back up to the house, Bee had gone home with her dad. I was glad the drama was over because it was only six days till the fair and there was work to do. To organise a successful swap stall *and* fill and sell one thousand water bombs was going to take all five of us.

five days to prepare the arsenal

My lips were bleeding. So were Fifty's. They looked dark red, like we'd been kissing vampires – Callum's description.

The water bombs arrived before I left for school, so we had five days to prepare a thousand. Fifty and me spent morning break and lunch break (apart from the eating part) filling them in the art room. We found a good way to tie the neck of the balloons but it involved forcing the end through the knot and then grabbing it with our teeth and yanking. The combination of the rubber and the water had, after a hundred bombs or more, made our lips raw. By afternoon break we'd had enough. When we got to our patch under the trees, Jonno was on the floor studying the creepy crawlies that he thinks are his friends, Bee was standing cross-armed and Copper Pie (who should have been helping) was messing about with a football.

'Get in here, Copper Pie,' Bee yelled, so loudly that the teachers in the staff room probably dropped their coffee cups.

'Right, Tribers. Today's Monday. The summer fair's on Saturday. I asked the Head if we could make posters and she said, "We can't have everyone plastering the walls of the school in posters, can we?" Is she mad? The Give and Take' (Bee had adopted my dad's suggestion) 'is the only environmentally responsible stall at the whole fair. Exactly *how* committed is she to the planet?'

Phew! Bee was in motormode.

'But it won't work if we don't let everyone know in advance – they won't bring anything to swap,' said Jonno.

'Exactly,' said Bee. 'So what do we do?'

'Spread the word in the playground,' said Jonno.

'Too random,' said Bee. 'It'll be like Chinese Whispers.'

I wasn't that interested. (And talking hurt my lips too much anyway.) Neither were Copper Pie and Fifty. We let Bee and Jonno rabbit on about how to advertise the swap stall.

'I've got to find someone with slimy lip stuff,' said Fifty. 'Any ideas?'

'You can ask Flo,' I said. 'She brings all sorts of pink pots to school.'

Fifty went off, and Copper Pie sloped away too. It wasn't like him to be so quiet but I wasn't worried about it. I should have been, but I wasn't.

four days till the bombs drop

It was all coming together nicely. Bribery was the answer. (But not the sort of bribery that got us in trouble over School Council elections.) No way could me and Fifty fill and tie a thousand water bombs, so we brought in some help. It was his idea. One free water bomb on the day of the fair for each ten filled, tied and put in the bucket. We were giving away the profits but who cared? There were six Year 5s in the art room with us and they worked while we watched.

Fifty's brain must have been working overtime because he said he'd also solved the swap stall problem. I didn't get a chance to find out how because Callum poked his head in.

'What do you want?' said Fifty.

'I want to know why you're playing with the little kids.' He meant our Year 5 workers.

'It's teamwork. Not something you'd know anything about, Hog.'

'Hog' is Copper Pie's name for Callum, because he hogs the ball in football.

'Looks like a sweat shop,' said Callum, before he disappeared along the corridor.

'So how have you solved the swap stall problem?' I asked.

'You'll find out soon enough.'

'Tell me, now.'

Bee and Jonno poked their heads round the door to see how we were getting on.

'Tell us what?' said Bee. She forced the idea out of him.

'You know the class list?' said Fifty.

We all nodded. Each class has one. It's emailed to the parents and has name, address, phone number and email address of everyone in your class so your parents can invite the whole lot to your birthday party even though (in my case) you only like four people.

'I emailed all the kids in our class who have a brother or sister in another class and got them to send me their list so now I've got the whole school. We don't need posters or Chinese Whispers. We can send an email about the Give and Take.'

As if the Head would let us do that? Fifty can be dim sometimes.

'Fantastic,' said Bee. 'I'll write the words, you send it.'

'No, not fantastic,' I said. 'There are rules about who can have your details and use them and all that . . .'

Oh no! I'd seen those looks before. The you're-such-a-drip ones.

One of the Year 5 workers stopped tying and said, 'He's right. Data protection. Unless all the parents crossed the box about sharing data you'll be in trouble.'

'How do *you* know?' said Fifty, looking down at him somehow even though the Year 5 was taller.

'My mum's an expert in data protection.'

'Well, don't tell her then,' said Bee.

'Or the deal's off,' added Fifty.

The worker went back to water-bomb assembly.

'Come on,' said Bee. 'You can leave them to it. Let's go and find Copper Pie and then we can have a go at the email. We need to get people to act. The swap stall's going to be huge.'

'Hey slaves,' said Fifty. 'We've got a meeting about the fair. Carry on and we'll be back before the end of lunch to count your bombs.'

It was good being managers. No chapped lips. No rubber taste in your mouth.

Bee found Copper Pie and dragged him away from his exciting game kicking the ball against the wall repeatedly, like a machine. We sat in our den listening to Bee make up advertising slogans to explain the stall.

'That's too many words,' said Jonno. 'It needs to be simple, and short.'

'Like Fifty,' said Bee. *Good one!*

'Watch it!' said Fifty.

'How about – get something for nothing,' said Jonno.

'It's not nothing though. It's get something for something else you don't want,' said Fifty.

'That's not snappy though, is it? Slogans are meant to be memorable.' Jonno was right.

'Something you want, for something you don't,' I said.

'Something you want, for something you don't,' Bee repeated. 'That's it, Keener.'

'Same,' said Fifty.

'We all agree,' said Jonno. 'Get sending, Fifty.'

'I'll do it as soon as I get home. Operation Email will be complete by 1700 hours.'

I was pleased I'd come up with the slogan, but that meant I was involved, which I wasn't pleased about. I avoid trouble like surfers on Solana Beach avoid great white sharks. The email was bound to come flying back at us – outraged parents, abusing the class list system, an unfair advantage, the data protection police . . .

'I'm going back to the art room before the bell goes. Coming, Fifty?'

'Sure.'

On the way I tried to talk him out of it. He doesn't like trouble either. But he was dead set on it.

'It's on your head,' I said, but it wouldn't be, would it? It would be on Tribe's.

* * *

I checked the computer before I went to bed. The email was there. And it was from Fifty, making him prime suspect if the Head found out. He could have at least used his mum's address.

> From: j.reynolds@bcffd.com
> Subject: SOMETHING YOU WANT, FOR SOMETHING YOU DON'T
> Date: 22 May 16:47:45 BST
> To: undisclosed-recipients
>
> At the summer fair on Saturday there is going to be a Give and Take stall. Please bring something you don't want, to swap for something you do.
> No money involved. This is an environmentally friendly stall.

three days until
the swap shop

We were all hanging around by the gates before school, except Copper Pie.

'Have you ever known Copper Pie be late? asked Fifty.

I thought about it. 'No,' I said.

'*Never*,' said Bee.

'He's probably trying to avoid the water bomb production line,' said Fifty.

'Has he even done one?' I asked.

'Don't think so,' said Fifty.

'How many are ready?' asked Bee.

I looked at Fifty to see if he knew. His face was blank, so I answered. 'About . . . four hundred?'

'So will you finish in time?'

'We will if we bribe some more kids,' said Fifty.

'I'll help,' said Bee. 'You will too, won't you, Jonno?'

'If I have to, but I'm going to make a lip shield first so I don't end up like them.'

He pointed at me and Fifty. Our lips had stopped bleeding but they were still a peculiar dark red colour, like we'd been gnawing raw meat.

Thanks to Bee's organisation, at lunchtime there were four Tribers (no Copper Pie – off sick according to Miss Walsh), three of the Year 5s from the day before (two were off sick, probably with lesser-known lip fever, and one had given up) and three new ones. In between bombs she told us how much stuff she'd already collected for the Give and Take, and how many kids had told her they were bringing cool things to swap.

'Don't forget we've got to go back to that lady who said she'd sort through her rubbish,' said Jonno (Swap Stall Deputy).

'Let's go after school,' said Bee. 'And then I need to

BEST ITEMS

Boomerang

French horn

Heart-shaped hot water bottle
  with no stopper

Mini darts set

Car seat with sticky patches

Set of skittles

New red and yellow stripy tights

Half of a pair of crutches

A typewriter

Pair of snow boots

Fruit bowl

An old-fashioned pram

do some cleaning. Some people are really disgusting – there's chewing gum on the French horn.' *Something sticky from someone else's mouth – yuck.*

'But what about the meeting?' I said. (It was Wednesday.)

'Let's postpone,' said Bee. 'Too much to do before Saturday.'

'Let's have a meeting after the summer fair instead,' said Jonno.

'Good idea, in the Tribehouse with cakes,' I said, remembering the fantastic marshmallow cupcakes Bee made to bribe the Alley Cat girls, ages ago when Tribe was new.

'Same,' said Fifty.

'There's no time to make any,' said Bee. *Shame!*

'I'll get Mum to buy some,' said Fifty.

Water bombs waiting in the art room, ready to burst, a pile of treasures in Bee's garage, ready to swap, and a tray of cakes waiting in the Tribehouse, ready to eat. It was all going too well . . .

'So here you all are,' said the Head. I had my back to her, so I stayed right where I was. Someone must have warned her about our factory – no prizes for guessing who.

'Who would like to explain this?' A piece of paper flapped behind my head. Something told me Operation Email was about to explode. Fifty was standing opposite me. He was trying hard not to confess, but it's hard to lie to the Head. He managed a few seconds, maybe even eight, of mouth-firmly-shut silence and then . . .

'It was me. I did it —'

But that was as far as he got.

'Fifty did it because *you* wouldn't let us put up posters and without posters no one would know to bring stuff to swap so our stall would be *ruined* and it's the only environmentally responsible stall at the whole fair and you're not supporting it even though you pretend to *care* about the planet.'

Oh no! Please will someone shut Bee up before she accuses the Head of being personally responsible for climate change.

Someone did: Jonno.

'What Bee means is that we're really committed to the recycling idea and as we couldn't do posters we . . . tried something else, and we're sorry if emails aren't allowed either, but I don't think we knew that rule, did we?' Jonno looked at the rest of us. Fifty and Bee shook their heads. I shook the back of mine. If there was a chance we might get away with it, we'll never know because . . .

Bee put her hands on her hips, looked through me at the Head and said, 'If the suffragettes had obeyed the *rules*, women wouldn't have the vote and *you* wouldn't be Head of our school, *you'd* be a housewife.'

I was so glad I couldn't see the Head's face. Her voice was enough. It was like a skewer and I was the kebab – all my major organs were pierced.

'You have been very rude, Beatrice. And the parallel with the women's movement is not valid in this case. Get up to

THE SUFFRAGETTES
BY BEE

They sound like a hip-hop band, don't they?

When my nan's nan was born women weren't allowed to vote in elections. (And black people weren't allowed to vote in America.) It's weird because everyone knows that's wrong so why did the governments allow it?

The Suffragettes were a group of women who protested and in 1918 they got the right to vote, but only if they were over 30 and had their own houses! That's still not fair so there was another rule made in 1928 and then men and women had the same rights. In America it took much longer for everyone to be equal. They could all learn from us – our Tribe is absolutely equal. Adults don't know much about being fair.

my office and wait there.'

Off she went, but the Head stayed.

'Amir, why are you helping to fill the water bombs for a Year 6 stall?'

'I'm a slave, Miss.'

That's all we needed: being accused of slavery. I put my head in my hands. Could things get any worse?

two days till
blast-off

Amazingly the Head sent Bee home. Fifty filled me in on the way to school the next day. He'd called her to check she was OK because she never came back to class. According to Fifty, Bee realised she was in deep deep trouble so she did the thing girls always do – she cried. *And* she told the Head her dad had left home. And that the email was her idea and she *made* Fifty do it.

I said, 'So if there are "family problems", you're allowed to be rude, have slaves, ignore the data protection rules and have the afternoon off. Result!'

That made Fifty mad. 'Keener, she *is* upset. You're the only one who doesn't seem to mind that Bee's mum and dad are probably going to divorce.'

'But I thought it was all better. I thought your mum . . . you know . . . waved her wand.'

'She did. And Bee's dad *is* back home but he still says the twins have to go. He's given them two weeks to find some-where else to live . . . or else.' He did the cutthroat sign.

Oh! I thought. And vowed to be a bit nicer. Especially as it was thanks to Bee we'd stormed through the water bombs and had less than a hundred left to do. That reminded me.

'What did the Head say about using Amir as a slave?'

'Stroke of luck there. Amir said it was only a joke – said he was helping out of the kindness of his heart.'

'Excellent.' I was worried we'd be in the poo for that.

'But he made Bee agree to double the rate for saying it: two free water bombs for every ten filled.'

'Fine by me,' I said. Filling the water bombs was a terrible job. That reminded me of something else: it was about time Copper Pie lent a hand.

'So what was wrong with Copper Pie yesterday?' I asked.

'I don't know. Didn't you ring him?'

'No,' I said. Normally I would have done, but with the fair, the email, slavery . . . I'd forgotten he was ill.

'He'll be at school today. He'd have to be dying from orange-hair fever for his mum to let him stay home two days.'

But he wasn't. Maybe he *had* contracted orange-hair fever. I texted him, but nothing came bleeping back.

Instead of a proper lesson, Miss Walsh asked us all to go through our plans for the fair.

'It's worth spending an hour now to make sure none of you forget anything essential on Saturday. We want to put on a good show for the parents, don't we?'

'Yes, Miss,' said Jamie. Callum's other half.

'Why don't we start with you then, Jamie? Who are you teamed up with?'

'I'm with Callum . . .' They're always together – no one else likes them. '. . . and Copper Pie.'

I must have misheard. And so must all the other kids in our class, who had their mouths hanging open. And so must Miss Walsh.

'Did you say you were with Callum *and* Copper Pie?'

Jamie nodded. And turned to smile at me, and then Fifty, and then Jonno and then Bee.

'Well, pop up here, Jamie and Callum. Copper Pie's off sick so you'll have to explain the stall without him.'

I didn't know what was going on but the one thing I knew for sure was that Copper Pie was *not* doing a stall with them. They were trying to wind us up. As soon as our fellow Triber was back at school he'd be on the water bombs, as agreed. And they'd be high on his list of victims.

'It's called Save or Score,' said Callum. 'I'm the goalie, Copper Pie's the scorer. If you score three goals against me, or save three shots from Copper Pie, you win a fiver. Jamie's doing the money.'

'That sounds excellent,' said Miss Walsh. 'We've talked about trying to pick a stall that uses your talents and you've clearly taken notice of that.'

They carried on talking about details: a sign, somewhere

to keep the money and rules about how close the shooter could get to the goal. I wanted to interrupt and explain that it wouldn't be happening, unless they found another shooter, but after the slave and suffragette comments Tribe didn't need more trouble. I made they're-completely-mental faces at the other Tribers instead.

Roddy did his and Harry's stall and then Bee stood up and introduced the Give and Take and Fifty did the water bombs.

'I trust you'll issue a health warning with each sale,' said Miss Walsh. 'We don't want soaked teachers, or parents.'

Fifty made a serious face. 'Absolutely, Miss. We wouldn't want that either.'

Alice went next. She gave a demonstration of her face painting, making Molly into a monkey. She said she'd been practising. It looked like someone had rubbed Molly's face in the mud.

It went on and on. The usual things: Lucky Dip, Splat the Rat, Stick the (Blu-Tack) Tail on the Donkey, Guess the Name of the Teddy.

If I'd stopped to think about it I might have wondered why we hadn't seen much of Copper Pie the week before the fair. But there was too much going on. Even when Callum and Jamie told us Copper Pie was doing a stall with them, I didn't believe there was anything wrong. My faith in my friend was one hundred percent. And the others felt the same.

We stood under the trees on our patch at break and this is how the conversation went:

Bee: 'Are they mad? Copper Pie with Callum – I don't think so.'

Jonno: 'Maybe they took advantage of the fact he's ill to make up a story.'

Me: 'As if we'd ever believe a Triber would pal up with enemy number one.'

Fifty: 'Same.'

Me: 'But I wish Copper Pie was here to tell them to get lost.'

Fifty: 'Same.'

Bee: 'I don't feel as though I've seen him all week, but I know I have.'

Jonno: 'He was away yesterday.'

Fifty: 'And the days he was here we were stuck in the art room.'

Me: 'And he was playing football.'

Fifty: 'He could have helped, couldn't he?'

Jonno: 'Do you blame him for not? You still look like you're wearing lipstick.'

Fifty: 'I'm never ever using my mouth as a tool again. It hurts to drink.'

Jonno: 'Talking of which, shouldn't we be finishing them off?'

Bee: 'No need. I've got a team in there doing it – *with* the Head's approval.'

Fifty: 'I don't know how you managed it but thank you, thank you.'

He went down on his knees and did fake weeping. Everyone started laughing and that was the end of that. It was two days until the fair. The water bombs were ready and we'd got away with the email. I was looking forward to raking in the money and spending some on the Splat the Rat. I wasn't even a teeny bit worried. Maybe if we'd talked about it some more we'd have realised something was up. If we'd put together the facts maybe we'd have worked it out. But we didn't. So on Friday, when I saw Copper Pie hanging around by the gates as usual, I was pleased to see my old friend back at school.

COPPER PIE'S FAMILY
(MUM, DAD, C.P., CHARLIE)
IN THE KITCHEN BEFORE SCHOOL

Dad: Do you *want* to be a professional footballer or not?

C.P.: I do. You know I do. But I can't do it, Dad.

Mum: Won't. He means won't.

Charlie: Mummy —

Mum: Shut up, Charlie.

Dad: All this fuss about a few water bombs.

C.P.: It's not about that. It's about doing the stall with Callum.

Dad: Nothing wrong with Callum. He's got a good eye for the ball.

C.P.: But he's not my friend.

Dad: We're talking about football here, boy. You don't have to hold his hand.

C.P.: But if I do the stall with Callum, I'll let *my* best friends down.

Mum: They'd let you down without a second thought, that lot.

C.P.: That's where you're wrong. They wouldn't. Ever.

Dad: Don't shout at your mother.

C.P.: She's shouting at me.

Dad: Listen. *You* are doing the Save or Score with

Callum and that's final. Simon's staying behind to watch you. When are you gonna get a chance like this again? He's a flipping football scout and instead of heading back up north to see his family he's STAYING BEHIND TO WATCH YOU. It's about priorities, boy.

Charlie: Daddy —

Dad: Shut up, Charlie boy. This is serious. I haven't told the school he's been sick and kept him home to practise so your big brother can mess about with water bombs. I haven't taken two days off work to stand in goal and coach your brother for nothing. Saturday could change his life. D'you hear me? Saturday could change his life.

summer fair
eve

'You'll never guess,' I said to Copper Pie.

'You'll never guess what those two morons have been saying about you,' said Fifty.

'You'll never guess the ridiculous story they've been putting about,' said Bee.

'You will never in a trillion years believe what Callum and Jamie have told the whole class,' said Jonno.

We waited for Copper Pie to ask us to tell him the crazy story . . . We waited for him to say, 'Spill, guys. What's been happening?' But he didn't. He looked at the floor. He moved a bit of dirt around with his foot. He put his hands in his pockets . . . and took them back out. Something was up. Even a geek like me could tell. Something was up.

'Don't you want to know?' said Jonno.

There was a silence where there should have been talking.

Goodbye, Copper Pie

'I think he already knows.' Fifty's five words were like five poison darts.

'I'd like to hear it from him,' said Bee, moving her hair out of her eyes and looking straight at Copper Pie. Her stare seemed to force his head up. And the answer was in his eyes.

'Why?' I said. 'Why would you . . .?'

My brain couldn't compute the data. Copper Pie would never team up with Callum. I needed to hear it from him, like Bee said.

'It's only a stall at the fair,' he said.

'No, it's not,' I said, loudly. 'It's . . .' I didn't know what it was. But it was bad, really bad.

'It's betrayal,' said Bee. 'You're out, Copper Pie. You're out of Tribe. If you go off with Callum, you're not one of us. You're not a Triber.'

He looked at us. We all shook our heads. Fifty was the first to turn away. Jonno and Bee followed, but I couldn't leave it like that.

'Copper Pie, why do you want to do it with Callum? I thought you were dead keen on the water bombs.' I paused to see if he would answer. He didn't. 'I know you love football but it's not worth it – losing Tribe to score a few goals at the summer fair.'

'I know, Keener. I do. But Dad's arranged for the scout to come and watch me. He set it all up. Rang Callum's dad so I had someone good to play against. I'm stuck in the middle.'

Do you know what empathy means? It means you

imagine what it would be like to be in someone else's shoes. I had a go. I tried to picture me, Keener, as a fantastic football player being given a chance to play in front of someone who could make me a champion. My feet were in Copper Pie's football boots but all I could see was Callum's sick grin and the Tribers on the sideline looking disgusted.

'Couldn't the scout watch you another day? When you're playing a proper match? That would be better, wouldn't it?'

'But he's hardly ever down this way. Dad says it's my only chance.'

If it was his *only* chance to be a star, maybe we *should* let him go off with the enemy?

I had another think. This time I tried to imagine it was me and *my* one chance of glory: world surfing champion Kelly Slater was coming to watch me, but to catch the surf when it was cooking and have a chance of riding a fat wave I had to leave Tribe. It didn't work, because I couldn't think why I'd ever have to leave Tribe and anyway the others would think it was super cool to be talent-spotted by a surf dude.

'Come on, Copper Pie,' I said.

'No. I'll stay here.' I didn't want to leave him there but I did. I left him kicking the dirt . . . and arrived at our patch at the same time as *Callum*.

'Hello Tribe. Looking forward to tomorrow? You can have a free go if you like. No chance of any of you winning a fiver against me and Copper Pie. But then you know how good he is, don't you? Because he's your mate.'

It was unbearable.

'Actually we're cool with it,' said Jonno. He really winds Callum up when he does that it's-no-big-deal thing.

'Liar,' said Callum, as he walked off.

'Well . . .' I said.

'Well what, Keener?' said Bee.

'I spoke to Copper Pie.'

'We got that. And?' I don't know why she was being stressy with me. *I* hadn't gone off with the enemy.

'And it's to do with the football scout.'

I explained but I could see the Tribers weren't about to run over and forgive him. And I could see why. As usual it was Jonno who put it into actual words.

'You know the thing is, if he'd told us about the scout and his dad's plan, we *might* have been all right about it, even though it's with Callum. But he didn't. He left Callum to tell us. That's not what friends do. And it's not what Tribers do.'

'I agree,' said Bee. 'He knew all week, I reckon. That's why he was avoiding us – kicking his ball and never tying water bombs. He's chicken.'

I didn't like her saying that. Copper Pie a coward!

'Same,' said Fifty. 'If he'd explained it to me *before*, I'd have said, "Go for it mate." After all, he can do a stall with Callum and still detest him. I mean, he plays football with him every week and that's never bothered us.'

'So what do we do?' said Bee.

No one said anything. It was too awful to think he had to leave.

'Let's wait,' said Jonno. 'Let's see if *he* does anything. He's the one who's deceived us.'

So we waited. We waited all day. He didn't come near our patch. He didn't say one word to any of us. I walked home with Fifty, and as he headed off to his house he said, 'Looks like this is it then. We're down to four Tribers. See you, Keener.'

'Bye,' I said. I felt really, really unhappy. The sort of unhappy that makes you forget you've ever laughed, or had fun, or caught an uncatchable wave, or been excited. I walked slowly home, thinking, thinking, thinking. And in a way it worked, because by the time I got home I knew something. I knew that I wasn't giving up on Copper Pie that easily. There were still twenty-two hours until the summer fair was declared officially open. That's what I knew.

lift-off
minus 22 hours

As I rocked from side to side in my hammock, thoughts went back and forwards and came back again. I was sure we could still be Tribe, as long as Copper Pie didn't *actually* go through with it. But how to stop him?

WAYS TO STOP THE SAVE OR SCORE

Break Copper Pie's leg (or any bone)

Break Callum's leg (or both of them)

Get the scout to cancel his visit

Get the summer fair cancelled - fire? (Fifty would love that. He could start it.)

Spill something poisonous on the goal

Hide the goal

Puncture every football within ten miles of school

Lock Copper Pie in the loos

Change Copper Pie's mind

If only I *could* change Copper Pie's mind.

'I'm going round to Copper Pie's,' I shouted.

I wasn't the only one. At the end of my road I turned left and there was Fifty's black curly hair bobbing along in front of me.

'Where are you off to?'

'Same place as you, I guess,' said Fifty.

'Great minds —'

'Think alike.'

We did the fist of friendship. I was glad there were two of us. Failure didn't seem so certain. And by the time we got to Copper Pie's road there was one more. Bee was hanging around on the corner.

'Hi guys.'

'What are you doing here, Bee?' said Fifty.

'I don't know . . . waiting, I suppose.'

'Waiting for what?' I said.

'For you, I suppose.' That didn't make any sense. We didn't know we were going to C.P.'s.

'But we didn't know we were coming,' said Fifty.

'Well, I must be controlling you then,' she said.

'So not funny, Bee,' said Fifty. 'You're here for the same reason we are. To rescue our idiotic friend from the dark forces that have lured him to the other side.'

'Maybe,' said Bee. 'But now that I'm here I don't know what to do.'

'Same,' said Fifty.

Goodbye, Copper Pie

I looked towards Copper Pie's house, hoping he might wander into the garden. I didn't fancy knocking on the door in case I got his mum.

'Shall we text him? Tell him to come out?' I said.

A red car roared past me at a hundred miles an hour, braked and swerved into Copper Pie's drive. Out stepped the football scout, Simon. Seeing him again made me realise what we were up against. There was no way Copper Pie was going to give up his chance of stardom.

'Let's go,' I said.

'I thought we were going to text?' said Bee. 'We might as well try.'

'There's no point,' I said, nodding my head towards the man standing on the doorstep. 'That's the scout.'

'He doesn't look very impressive,' said Fifty.

'He doesn't have to, does he? He's not the one who kicks the ball,' said Bee.

'Come on,' I said. I'd seen enough. We were no match for a top scout and a football-mad dad.

Later, in bed, all I could think was that we'd decided no one can leave Tribe and no one can join. That's what we decided. So was it the end? Was Tribe finished?

a
sell-out

It all happened according to plan (as long as you ignored the fact that there were only four of us).

The water bombs went down a storm, as predicted. We lined up the buckets of bombs by our table and made everyone queue in a zigzag (otherwise the queue would have wrapped round three other stalls). Amir went off to get more stock from the art room every time we ran out (we paid him obviously). We sold our first one to Lily at 2.01 p.m. and our last one to Flo's friend, Joe, at 2.22 p.m. Allowing for the ones we had to give away as payment, and the ones we accidentally burst, and the ones we had for free, we made £73.19. (Quite how we ended up with nineteen pence I don't know.) We could have sold more – there were plenty of people to aim for! I was lucky enough to see a high lob explode right on top of the Head's hairdo. Miss Walsh got one in the face and Mr Morris was attacked from three directions in a co-ordinated attack. Flo got a soaking too. (Who would do a thing like that!) All the kids bought one, except Copper Pie, who was too busy (and wouldn't have dared come up even if he hadn't been).

The swap stall didn't last long either. The whole of the table was piled high with tat (Jonno's word: means things no one needs) apart from where Flo's supermarket till sat (for the water bomb money). But from the minute the gates opened there were five rows of people all trying to grab stuff. Bee and Jonno tried to control what was given and what was taken in exchange (to make sure no one *gave* a mouldy tennis ball and took a brand new skateboard – not that there was one) but it was bedlam. Alice and a Year 3 girl had a tug-of-war over a sparkly skipping rope, Mr Morris swiped a butterfly net from some kid that thought it was a fishing net and two little boys had a scrap over a pottery wheel. (No point. Flo had one. It never worked.) Anonymous hands kept appearing from behind bodies and snatching. And there was shouting:

I saw that first.

Pass me the orange rubbery thing.

Is it for cooking?

Urghh! It's all sticky.

It's a tea cosy, not a hat. Idiot – it's a hot water bottle cover.

Get off. That's not a swap. It's my walking stick.

And then someone spotted the old-fashioned pram, filled it up to the top with stuff from the stall and sauntered off without giving anything. *That* was the final straw. Bee chased after her. We all watched.

'Excuse me. The idea of our stall is that you *donate* something you don't need any more and *take* something in its place.' Bee stared down at the pramful of loot.

'Sorry, love,' said the woman. She put her hand in her jeans pocket and pulled out a 50p piece. 'There you go.'

Bee was stunned, and for once, lost for words. The pram lady wandered off. Back at the stall the Give and Take had turned into more of a Shove and Steal. Poor Jonno got elbowed in the face by someone lunging for the French horn, and clonked on the head by a fruit bowl that someone was trying to pass to an old man at the other end.

'Let's leave them to it,' he said.

'We can't,' said Bee. 'They'll take everything.'

'Isn't that the point?' he said.

Just then the lady who'd taken the pram appeared back at the stall. I had a good look at her in case she was a professional thief and the police needed a report: jeans, green jumper, parrot earrings.

'I'll take the lot off you for a tenner,' she said.

'No way,' said Bee. 'This is about recycling. It's not for sale.'

'Are you joking?' she said. 'Listen to her, Ray.' She nudged the man next to her. I stopped serving so I didn't miss what was coming.

'We'll give you twelve quid. Put it in your recycling tin,' he said.

Jonno held out the fruit bowl that the old man at the end had put back. 'Twenty-five pounds and it's all yours. It's worth at least that.'

'What are you doing, Jonno?' Bee hissed.

'Getting rid of this lot – they don't care about the planet.'

I scanned the crowd – it was still three deep. People grabbing things with their sticky fingers, dropping them, putting them back, picking them up again, desperately trying to get the plastic flowers or the soap dish before someone else did.

'I'm with Jonno,' I said.

'Same,' said Fifty.

'Twenty,' said Ray.

'Twenty-five and I'll throw in the fruit bowl,' said Jonno.

'No. Twenty's my top.'

'Strictly speaking you still owe us for the pramload *she* took earlier,' said Bee.

Ooh! It was getting nasty.

'I paid you,' she said.

'50p. Big deal. It's people like you —'

'I'd stop there if I were you,' said Ray.

'We didn't come here to be insulted.' The woman's parrot earrings began to swing wildly

'Why did you come then?'

'Leave it, Bee. Twenty-five pounds and I'll put it all in boxes for you,' said Jonno.

Bee turned round and walked off with her nose in the air. Jonno put his hand out for the money. Everyone was waiting to see if Ray was going to pay up. He reached into his back pocket, pulled out a wad of notes and peeled off two tens and a five.

'Thanks,' said Jonno, and passed it to me. 'And what about all the stuff in the pram? A fiver?'

'You're joking.'

'No.'

'Give him the money,' said a girl's voice in the second row.

Jonno held his palm out again.

'Hand it over,' yelled Fifty.

'Be fair. They're only kids,' said someone else.

Ray looked at the woman. He didn't seem to know what to do.

'I saw her take the pram. It was full to the top with brilliant things,' said a familiar voice. 'It was full to ten pounds.'
Well done, Flo!

Being accused by a cute (if you don't know her) little girl was too much for Ray.

'Daylight robbery . . . Another tenner it is then. But for that I want it all packed up and brought over to my car. It's the navy Range Rover.' He pointed to the shiny tank parked across two spaces. I was glad Bee wasn't there or they'd have had an argument about 4x4s polluting the planet.

'Will do,' said Jonno. He turned to the crowd. 'Stall's shut, sorry.'

No one seemed to mind the sudden closure. I think

they'd all enjoyed the show.

'Well done,' said Fifty. 'You stood your ground.'

'Thanks, but why did he want all this junk?' said Jonno.

'To sell at a car boot sale,' said Fifty. 'It's big business.'

'Good luck to them.'

'Same.'

While me and Fifty were busy selling, and Bee was shouting, and Jonno was negotiating, the fact that Copper Pie was scoring goals right in front of us didn't seem so terrible. But as soon as the table was cleared and delivered to the Range Rover and the water bomb buckets were empty, the horrible feelings of betrayal came back, twice as bad. Bee and Jonno had a walk round the other stalls and then sat under our table. I didn't even bother with the walking round, not even to splat a rat.

'Keener, why's Copper Pie playing with Callum?' said Flo. That was all I needed. I thought about making up some stupid answer but I couldn't be bothered so I told her the truth.

She was excited. Trust her. 'Which one's the scout, Keener?'

'I don't know,' I said. *Where is the scout?* I thought.

It was 3.07 p.m. and there was no sign of Simon of the big white trainers and the red car.

'Fifty, have you seen the scout anywhere?'

'Nope.'

* * *

I didn't move from my spot for the next fifty-three minutes. I kept watch. I was pretty sure Copper Pie was doing the same. A couple of times I caught his eye but he pretended I hadn't. I was absolutely sure that the scout hadn't turned up. And neither had Copper Pie's dad. But I wasn't pleased. There was no 'ha ha serves you right'. Inside, even after what he'd done to Tribe, I wanted him to have a chance at being Ronaldo, or Ronaldo Junior . . .

The raffle prizes were announced and the Head, whose hair was still wet, declared the fair over (and a great success). Bee handed over the £35.50 from the car-boot man and his pram-stealing wife. Fifty handed in our £73.19. (Dad said we didn't need to pay him back for the water bombs. It was his contribution.) We put the buckets back in the art room and left.

I was really miffed. All this fuss. Tribe in pieces. All for nothing. More than anything I wanted everything to go back to normal. But I'd never get the others to agree. Scout or no scout, Copper Pie had left us in the lurch. I went off with Bee, Fifty and Jonno to the Tribehouse for cakes as agreed, but I didn't want one. I wanted to find a way to put it all right. I was still cross with my oldest friend, but not so cross that I didn't want to be his mate. No . . . not that cross.

cakes at
the Tribehouse

'The Head said ours was the most successful stall,' said Jonno as we walked down Fifty's street.

'Depends what you mean by success, doesn't it?' said Bee.

'She means money.'

'Money sounds like success to me,' said Fifty.

'It would,' said Bee. 'But selling out to a car-boot king wasn't what I had in mind.'

'Loads of people got great swaps before the pram thief bought everything,' said Jonno.

'It wasn't only the pram thief's fault,' said Fifty. 'Everyone was pushing and shoving.'

'You'll be telling me I should thank the pram thief next,' said Bee.

'You know, Bee, you should be thanking the pram thief!' said Fifty.

I let them ramble on. Didn't they care about Copper

Pie? Were we really about to have the Tribe meeting with cakes but without a ginger nut?

We went through the cat flap. I was last and by the time I got into the garden the Tribers had frozen like musical statues again! Bee pressed her finger against her lips. 'Shhhushhh ...'

'We've seen feet,' whispered Fifty.

This time I *knew* it was a joke. There couldn't be another uninvited guest in our hut. I ignored them and went up to the door – totally confident that the Tribehouse was empty. But before I went in, I glanced down, to check that where the door doesn't fit properly, light was shining under as normal. Something wasn't quite right. There was light, but it was stripy – light/shade/light/shade/light. It looked like there were two blocks in the way, like ... legs.

'Shhushhh,' I said. *What else could be blocking the light?* The safe? *No.* A new chair with very fat legs that Fifty's mum put in there to surprise us? *No.* I stepped back, on to Fifty, and knocked him flying. (It's a hazard, him being so small.) He squeaked.

'Shhhushhh. There really *is* someone in there,' I said, and ran ... I'd like to say that I knew the Tribers were right behind me but actually I didn't care. If it was a monster – one with lots of heads – I didn't want to be there to see it.

'At last,' said a voice I'd heard before. 'I've got better things to do than hang around in garden sheds for some kids that are nothing but trouble.'

The monster was Copper Pie's dad.

still cakes at
the Tribehouse
(because the cakes hadn't been eaten yet)

'Err . . . hello,' said Fifty.

'Your mum's not in so I waited here,' said Copper Pie's dad. 'Thought you'd all turn up eventually. I've been sent to get you.'

'By who?' said Bee.

'By the boss, that's who.'

'Which boss exactly?' said Fifty.

'The wife. Copper Pie's mum.'

'She wants us?' said Bee.

'She does,' said Copper Pie's dad.

'Could I ask why?' said Fifty, being ultra-polite.

'To sort out this mess, of course.'

'With Copper Pie?' said Jonno.

'That would be it.'

'What about Callum?' said Bee, with ice in her voice.

'He's gone off in a right mood.'

'Because the scout didn't turn up?' said Jonno.

'He did turn up,' said Copper Pie's dad. 'A bit late, that's all.'

'Too late,' I said.

'That's why you've got to come over. It's my fault Copper Pie didn't get his chance, so the wife says. And it's my fault you lot have fallen out, so Copper Pie says. Now, I don't need all this fuss so you need to come with me and sort it out.'

I didn't know what the other Tribers were thinking but I didn't want to go. I wanted us to be friends, but not because C.P.'s mum and dad bullied us into it.

'Sorry,' said Bee. 'We're having cakes and then I've got to go home. It's not our fault Copper Pie went off with Callum and left Tribe to —'

'Rot,' said Fifty. I was thinking of 'stew'.

'No, it's my fault. I just said that. And the cakes can wait because I'm not going back without you lot, and that's that.' Copper Pie's dad wasn't taking 'no' for an answer.

'OK,' said Jonno.

'Same,' said Fifty.

'Doesn't look like I've got a choice,' said Bee. She narrowed her eyes.

'Bee, that face could kill a crow,' said Copper Pie's dad. I'd never heard that expression before but I liked it.

We all clambered into Copper Pie's dad's van. Bee sat in the front.

Goodbye, Copper Pie

'So how's your dad?' Copper Pie's dad asked Bee.

'He's at home for now. But the twins have only got till next Wednesday to find somewhere else to live or he's off again.'

'That's a rum deal,' said Copper Pie's dad.

'For who?' said Bee.

'For the lot of you. It's not fair on you or your mum, but your dad's got a point. Those brothers of yours are old enough to fly the nest.'

Bee *always* sticks up for her mum, but not this time. She stayed quiet.

'Excuse me,' said Fifty from the back. 'Why didn't the talent scout come?'

A big sigh. 'Everything that could go wrong, did. The game kicked off late. The parents of the player Simon was interested in wanted a word that turned into a blinking book and then we got stuck in a queue behind an over-turned caravan. Crawled along for two hours.'

'Not your fault then,' said Jonno.

'No. Not that bit. But I'm definitely in the frame for the rest. That Charlie's on your side too, even though his brother tortures him. Last time I interfere – Copper Pie can be a dustman for all I care. Waste of a good left-footer, though.'

Copper Pie's dad cut the engine. We were there. But no one got out.

'Come on.'

We went in through the back door. Charlie was having a

snack. It looked like Marmite spread on raw carrot. Copper Pie's mum was washing up.

'Hi Charlie,' I said.

'Heyyo Keener. Can we pway marble wun?'

'In a minute maybe.'

'Copper Pie! Get down here,' shouted his mum.

We waited.

'What's that, Charlie?' said Bee.

'Ca-wots.'

'And what's the brown stuff?'

'Choc-yit sauce.'

'Nice,' said Fifty.

Copper Pie shuffled in, and his trainers made a squeaky rubber noise as they scraped along the chessboard floor. I was worried he'd leave black streaks on the white squares but I didn't spot any. I waited for his shouty mum to tell him to pick his feet up.

'You've made your point,' said Copper Pie's dad. 'Pick those feet up and stop the wounded soldier act. I've brought your friends.'

C.P. jerked his head up and we locked eyes. I smiled. I mean, I don't want to go on and on, but he is my oldest friend. What would you do?

'Hi there,' I said.

He nodded.

'Go on then, Keener,' said Copper Pie's dad. 'Tell him it's all forgotten and forgiven.'

Goodbye, Copper Pie

But it isn't, I thought. I had a quick recce to see what the others were expecting me to say. It was hard to tell. Bee looked mean. Jonno looked normal (I mean the same as he usually does, which is actually not normal at all: big mad hair, specs falling off his nose). Fifty looked uncomfortable. Copper Pie's mum looked scary (the same as normal). His dad was smiling at me in an encouraging way. I needed some time to think things through. The Tribers were still miffed with Copper Pie so I couldn't say everything was all right, because it wasn't. Say nothing – that seemed the best idea, even though it's rude not to answer.

If only someone else would speak . . .

'Keener, can we pway the marble wun now pwease?'

Thank you, Charlie!

'OK,' I said. 'Shall we do it in your room?' I was already reaching for the box and heading for the door.

'Yes pwease,' said Charlie.

'You coming?' I said to the others. Copper Pie had no choice – I grabbed his elbow on my way out of the kitchen. Charlie followed. (He is probably the nicest person in the family.) I hoped the others would come. Surely the Tribers all wanted us to be back together? Especially as Copper Pie's dad had said everything was his fault. Copper Pie didn't *want* to play with Callum. He was bullied into it.

'Sorry about the scout,' I said, as we headed for the stairs.

'Dun't matter,' said Copper Pie.

'It does matter,' I said. 'I was hoping to be your manager

or chauffeur or something and have loads of money and all that.'

He thumped me. *Why does he do that?* I don't like pain. Everyone knows that.

'I'd never employ you. I'd have fat guys in shiny suits and shades looking after me.'

I laughed. Not because it was funny. But because we were chatting for the first time in what seemed like *forever*.

'Can I be the dwi-ver?' said Charlie.

'If you can reach the pedals, maybe.' That was the nicest thing I'd ever heard C.P. say to his brother. Charlie smiled a big cheesy smile.

I made it up the stairs without tripping on any of the latest obstacles: a satsuma skin, a Lego Indiana Jones, a bucket, one roller blade and a dummy, sat on the floor and started making Charlie's marble run. No one else came up.

'So will the scout come another day?'

'I don't reckon so.'

'Why not?'

'He says I'm too young really. Need a few more years before a proper club would take me on.'

'He should have said that before. Then you could have done the water bombs and you wouldn't be the outcast Triber.'

I meant it as a joke but when I heard it out loud it didn't sound funny. It sounded serious. It sounded final.

'Am I out then?' said my ginger friend who saved me

from Annabel Ellis and ate all the bits of lunch I didn't like *every* day.

"Course not,' I lied.

'How come you're the only one up here then?'

'I'm here,' said Charlie.

'You don't count. You wear a nappy.'

Charlie looked down at his nappy and started to peel off the sticky bit at the side.

'No, no, no,' I said. 'You do count, Charlie. Really.'

He went back to plopping marbles down the three runs that I'd made interconnect. It was hypnotising. Either that or I was busy trying to avoid the subject of Tribe.

'D'you think they've gone home?' said Copper Pie. He was trying to sound normal but inside he was sick – I could tell. Sick at the thought that he wasn't a Triber any more.

Yes, I do, I thought but I didn't say it. I mean, they were hardly going to be having tea and scones downstairs with Shouty Shouty.

'So you're an outcast too then?'

I hadn't thought of that. Did siding with Copper Pie make me a non-Triber? A panicky feeling came over me. I wanted us *all* to be friends again. But if being with Copper Pie meant I wasn't friends with Jonno, Bee and Fifty then I wasn't ready for that.

two giant yellow
rubber gloves

I jumped up and ran downstairs. I had to know what had happened to the others. I stopped at the bottom of the stair-case – I could hear the Tribers laughing. That wasn't what I was expecting.

Were they laughing at the way I'd trotted off with Copper Pie, like a pet, after everything he'd done?

Something stopped me going in. Worry, I suppose. I try not to worry any more. I try and chase away all the horrible thoughts by making up rubbish words. Anything to keep the worry bit of my brain occupied.

Bee's voice rang out. 'It's Keener.'

More laughter. I pricked up my ears, like a dog.

'Total nerd.' That was Fifty. So much for friends. They were laughing about me behind my back. Cowards.

Coward is a horrible word. I decided not to be one. They'd obviously ganged up together and I was the one they were having a go at. Well, they could say it to my face. I barged in. But no one noticed me. They were too busy studying something on the kitchen table. Copper Pie's parents were nowhere to be seen. I coughed.

'Keener, just in time. Look at this one.'

Fifty made a space so I could see. *Oh great!* That was all I needed. A photo of me in Reception, with my hands in two giant yellow rubber gloves. Ha ha. So I didn't like glue. Who cares?

The table was covered in old photos. I saw a flash of orange and green: Copper Pie in a Tyrannosaurus Rex costume. Classic. I could feel a grin starting. I remembered that birthday party. I was sick on the way home.

'Who's that?' said Jonno, pointing at a picture of a little boy dressed up as a ladybird.

A guffaw exploded from somewhere deep inside. I managed to squeeze out, 'It's Fifty.' Fifty's hair was like a ginormous black woolly hat and his cheeks were all rosy.

'You should have been a girl,' said Bee, grabbing it.

'So cute,' said Jonno.

'Wait till you see Bee. She was a giraffe. She must be in one of them.' Fifty started shuffling all the photos. 'Here she is.'

'Too much,' said Jonno, holding his middle. Bee's face was poking out of the middle of some spotty brown fur. She didn't have any hair because it was all tucked up into the giraffe head.

'What's so funny?' said Copper Pie, to our backs.

I held up the dinosaur pic.

'That was my animal birthday party,' he said. 'Let's see.' He took it. The table was like a diary of our lives. There was every party, every Christmas play (Bee as an angel!), the time we went sledging in bobble hats and mittens using trays and bin bags, Charlie's christening (with me holding him and Bee feeding him a bottle). We had to explain everything to Jonno, the only Triber who wasn't around to see it all. I don't know how long we sat there but eventually, when we'd been through the lot, someone said they were hungry and we remembered the cakes at the Tribehouse. Bee packed the photos away in the shoebox and put it back on the top of one of the cupboards.

'Let's go,' she said. 'To the Tribehouse!'

'Come on, Copper Pie,' said Fifty.

He looked at the Tribers, one at a time.

'Am I still in? Still a Triber?'

'Looks like it,' said Bee. 'I can't see any pictures of Callum in your mum's box so I reckon you must be one of us.'

'I didn't want to do it. Dad made me.'

'We know,' said Fifty. He paused then added, 'Now.'

'You could try talking to us next time,' said Jonno.

'There won't be no next time,' said Copper Pie.

I chose a cake with a Flake on top. It was absolutely delicious. Helped by the fact the Tribers were in the Tribehouse, all together again.

'She's clever, your mum,' said Jonno.

'That's not what most people say,' said Copper Pie. 'Most people say she shouts.'

'But she got out that box, didn't she? And everyone remembered how long you've been friends and all the stuff you've done together. She helped sort it out.'

'I s'pose.'

'I wish I had old friends.'

We all looked at Jonno. Who was as much a part of Tribe as all of us, even though we'd only known him a few weeks. Fifty put it into words.

'Once you join, you can't leave. Even if you disappear for a while with our number one enemy, like Copper Pie here, you're still a Triber. So you'll have old friends, Jonno. You'll have us, till you die.'

'Unless we go first,' said Bee.

'Can we not talk about dying?' I said. 'Can we just eat the rest of the cakes?'

Copper Pie flopped his hand down. We all followed. The Tribe handshake said it all.

Show
and Tell

Bee's mum
is sad

We were on our way home from school.

'I love Tuesdays,' I said. It's the day we do D.T. 'All I need is a layer of glaze to make it shiny and my Spitfire will be finished. I can't wait.'

'Good for you,' said Fifty. His fire engine looked more like a vandalised post box. 'I can't wait to burn mine.'

'You can burn mine too,' said Copper Pie. His chip van mysteriously got crushed between lessons. (We suspected Jamie, working on Callum's orders.) Bee finished hers ages ago. She chose a boat for her vehicle, which was a good idea because wheels are difficult.

We stopped halfway down the alley to chat to Sass who's this really cool girl at the senior school. We used to be scared of her but ever since we gave her and her mates some cupcakes, made by the one and only *Bee the Baker*, she's been a mate.

'Hey Tribers, how goes it?'

'Good,' said Jonno.

'Were you at the fair?' said Bee. 'I thought I saw you.'

'Yeah, Mum made me take my brother. He spent the whole time trying to score against that goalie. I saw you guys with a table full of —'

'Rubbish,' said Fifty.

'I'd have come over but . . .' She shrugged. 'Anyway, it looked like there was trouble brewing.'

'Trouble's one word for it,' said Jonno. 'War would be the other.'

Sass laughed. I think Jonno *really* likes her — if you get what I mean.

'We gave up and sold the stall in the end,' said Bee.

Fifty finished off the story. 'This car-booter with wads of cash took the lot off us for thirty-five quid.'

'You lot always manage to swing things your way. How d'ya do it?'

We grinned at each other.

'OK. I get it,' she said. 'It's the Tribe thing.'

She walked with us to the other end of the alley where we almost ran straight into . . . Bee's mum.

'What are you doing here?' said Bee.

I'd never seen her mum anywhere near school before. As far as I can make out she's either at work, or cooking, or shopping.

'They've gone.' Bee's mum started sniffing.

'Who've gone, Mum?'

'The boys.' Proper crying started. *Time for a quick exit.* I grabbed Fifty's arm. Copper Pie didn't need grabbing, he'd already sloped off round the corner. Sass had disappeared too.

'See you tomorrow, Bee,' I shouted. 'Come on, Jonno.'

Jonno didn't come. Jonno has an annoying habit of not coming! We waited out of sight for a few minutes.

'What's Jonno up to?' said Fifty.

'No idea,' said C.P.

'Surely he's not going to walk home with Bee's wailing mum?' Fifty made a surely-not face.

'I hate it when my mum cries,' I said.

'Same,' said Fifty.

'My mum never cries,' said Copper Pie. 'I think she was born without the right bits.'

'Tear ducts,' I said.

'That'll be it,' said Copper Pie. 'No tear ducts.'

'I reckon my mum got your mum's,' said Fifty. 'She cries at everything. If you said: imagine there was a little puppy and it trod on a drawing pin, that would be it – she'd be off, box of tissues, red eyes.'

'But that is quite sad,' I said, and wished I hadn't. Copper Pie called me girly.

Thankfully Jonno reappeared.

'Why did you all disappear? Bee's our friend.'

'But Bee's mum isn't,' said Fifty. Jonno made a face so Fifty quickly added, 'But we like her of course. And she makes a good lasagne.'

TRIBERS' SAD THINGS
(SOME OF THEM AREN'T SAD THOUGH)

Winters with no snow

Batteries running out when you're playing some
thing

Less than 3500 Black Rhinos left on the planet
(Bee's very sad about that)

No pudding

No loo roll and no one to get you any

Fire alarms with no fire (only Fifty thinks that's
sad)

Waking up too early on Christmas morning

The day after Christmas (364 days to wait)

Getting woken up from a nice dream

Not getting woken up from a bad dream

Dropping your book in the bath (only Keener thinks
that's sad)

'What's up anyway?' said Copper Pie.

We walked along as Jonno explained.

'Remember when Bee's dad said the twins had two weeks to get out?'

'Yes.' I did remember, but I hadn't actually thought about it since. My mum and dad are always threatening things they don't end up doing.

'Well, they've gone already. And Bee's mum is seriously upset.'

'I don't get why,' said Fifty. 'It's normal to leave home when you've left school. No way will I live with my mum when I grow up.'

'You might never grow up,' said Copper Pie. 'You might stay fifty percent smaller than everyone else, *forever*.'

Fifty kicked him. Copper Pie slapped him round the head and turned to run away. Fifty jumped on his back. They're always messing.

'Where have her brothers gone?' I asked.

'They're renting a room from an *actress*,' said Jonno.

'A real actress?' said Fifty.

'No, a cartoon one.' Fifty dissed by Jonno – I liked it.

'Where is it?' I asked.

'The house is in Stoke Park. Wherever that is.'

'It's an estate,' I said. 'Quite new, with a grassy bit in the middle.'

'Bee's mum says their house feels too empty without the twins,' said Jonno. 'That's why she came to meet Bee.'

'There's no such thing as too empty,' said Fifty. 'What would I give to be home alone?'

'Without your baby sister?' I said. 'Come on, Fifty. We all know she's your all-time favourite person.'

'I meant without Mum and Dad. Probably Rose can hang out with me anytime. We could make a fire and sing songs while we toast marshmallows.'

Probably Rose is quite cute, unlike my little sister, Flo, who's irritating and tells lies.

'Anyway, they've gone to the dodgy café for a cup of tea,' said Jonno.

The dodgy café has a tattoo parlour in the back. If you go in there without a drawing of a snake or an eagle on your arm you feel a bit like you've forgotten to put your pants on – according to Sass that is. I've only ever peeked through the window.

When I got in from school Mum was on the phone. Flo was at the kitchen table, eating a teacake and drinking some apple juice. There was some left out for me too. I sat down with her and scoffed. For once Flo was completely quiet. It was bliss. I left her and went up to my room to make a space for the Spitfire that was coming home soon. It took a lot of rearranging to find a suitable spot.

'Te-ea,' shouted Mum.

It was fish cakes, pasta and peas. Mum, Flo and Amy had pesto too but I don't like it. (Dad gets home late in the week and eats on his own.) I sat down and started eating.

'So Flo, how was school?' asked Amy. She's turning into a second mum.

Flo shrugged her shoulders. Something was up. She normally talks the whole time – not even a mouthful of mashed potato stops her.

'Did you not get chosen for Show and Tell again?' said Mum.

Flo shook her head. *That* explained the silence. She'd taken Fat Cat. She made him from two woolly pom-poms and two cardboard triangles (for ears) and then she felt-tipped-on whiskers that looked like scribble. It was rubbish. She's always taking weird things. No wonder she never gets picked.

'Never mind,' said Amy. There was another long silence.

'Did anyone bring anything good?' asked Mum.

Flo shook her head again.

REALLY BAD SHOW AND TELLS
TRIBERS REMEMBER FROM YEAR 3

Home-made knitted scarf for a teddy
Home-made knitted hat for a teddy
Hospital identification bracelet with spots of blood
Snack pack of dried jellyfish from Japan
Fossil that was actually a stone
Tooth, with bits of Weetabix left on
Blurred photo of someone's dog
Certificate for swimming 5 metres
Panning for gold medal from Legoland
Eggcup from Torquay

Amy and Mum swapped she's-being-moody-and-spoilt looks and Amy started going on about her boyfriend instead. Mum listened to her endlessly dull rabbiting and then said what she always says: 'Just make sure you don't get *too* serious about him, Amy.' What I think she means is: Can't you find one that's not so spotty?

'Aren't you hungry?' Mum asked. Me and Amy had finished and were on pudding but Flo still had half a plate full of pasta.

'Not really,' said Flo.

'OK. You can get down,' said Mum. 'And maybe you'll get chosen to show Fat Cat next time.'

Let's hope not, I thought. Fat Cat really wasn't something to show off about.

Bee's mum is mad

Bee was late for school.

'We'd given up on you,' said Fifty at break.

'I've given up on my mum,' said Bee.

'Oh! Is she still upset?' said Fifty. He was trying to be nice but Bee wasn't in the mood.

'What do you think, Fifty? That Mum was crying yesterday but today she woke up ecstatically happy? Duh!'

Fifty raised his eyebrows. They're like two thick black slugs. (He can lift one at a time, and turn his tongue over, and turn his eyelids inside out.) I raised my almost-invisible-because-they're-so-blond ones back at him. The message was clear: Bee was stressy.

'Your mum'll get used to your brothers not being there,' said Jonno. *Brave!* I waited for Bee to snap his head off.

'But will I?' said Bee. 'It's so strange. There's nothing to . . . clear up, or trip over, and the fridge is full, and the telly's off for the first time in my whole life. Mum followed me around like a shadow *all* last night. And Dad's back but not forgiven. Mum keeps throwing him evil looks.'

You can never really understand what's going on in someone else's head. I understood what she was saying, but had no idea how it felt. If my sisters left home I'd be in heaven. No teasing. No silly girl-talk at tea. No weird boyfriend coming round all the time. No dollies. No lumps of long matted-together hair that look like spiders in the plughole. I could go on . . .

'How are you getting on with the Earth Day plan?' said Jonno. He was trying to distract Bee. And it worked.

'You'll never guess who's going to take it over when we leave?' she said. We didn't even try.

'Tell us,' said Fifty.

'Amir,' she said.

'You're joking,' said Jonno. 'He's not into the planet. He's into making deals.'

'That's the mistake people make,' said Bee. 'They think if you're green, you're all . . . wishy-washy. But to get the message across you need to be . . .' She couldn't find the words, but Fifty did.

'A smooth operator.'

'Exactly,' she said.

I hardly saw her for the rest of the day. She was in a huddle with Amir and another kid that helped us with the water bombs. I was glad that was all over. Tribe needed a bit of peace. Time to do stuff just for us, for Tribe. I mean, we still hadn't made our ID cards. It was time for another one of my lists. I decided to make one after school, before the Wednesday meeting.

There was a dog at the school gates. Nothing unusual about that, except the lead was attached to the wrist of Bee's mum, who doesn't have a dog. Equally unusual was the fact that, for the second day running (and the second day ever), Bee's mum had come to meet Bee.

'Mum, what's that?'

'It's Doodle. Say hello to him.'

She didn't. She stared.

Fifty said it instead. 'Hello Doodle.' He looked just like the dog, black and fluffy. He wasn't much taller either, as Doodle showed us when he jumped up at him.

'Get off!' Fifty shuffled backwards. Doodle snapped at him.

'Don't do that, Doodle,' said Bee's mum, stroking his nose. Doodle grabbed the side of her hand in his teeth. She had to grab his top jaw and prise it open. Doodle wasn't making a very good impression.

'Mum, where did he come from and when's he going back?'

Doodle tried to jump up at Bee, but Bee's mum pulled him back, half strangling the poor puppy.

'Sit! Doodle.'

Doodle laid down and started gnawing the corner of Copper Pie's sports bag.

'He's our puppy, Bee. Isn't that exciting?'

I looked over at Copper Pie. He was making a she's-doolally face.

'Mum, it's not exciting, it's mad. We can't have a puppy. We don't need one. We don't have room for a puppy, or time to walk it, or anything.' Bee sounded desperate. I'd have felt the same. Who would want to share a house with that black beast's teeth?

'Of course we have room. Doodle will help fill the hole left by your brothers.' Bee's mum's eyes went all teary as she stroked Doodle's head. Doodle had another go at eating her hand.

Bee rolled her eyes. I didn't see her do it because her fringe was covering them but I could tell by the way her mouth moved. Jonno bent down and gave Doodle a rub on his back.

'Hello boy,' he said. 'You're a lovely doggy, aren't you? You're a Labradoodle.'

Doodle went for Jonno's fingers but Jonno was too fast. He whipped his hand away and turned his face away too, as though he was ignoring Doodle (which I thought was a bit mean as he'd just said what a lovely dog he was). Doodle jumped up at Jonno but Jonno acted like he wasn't there, turning away from him again. Weird. *Who cares?* I was ready to go. Dogs aren't my thing (dribble, sharp teeth and claws, poo, hair, yucky smells). Copper Pie and I strolled off.

'Bye, Bee. See you at the meeting,' I shouted. Fifty followed, but Jonno stayed with the dog, which he was ignoring.

'Are you coming?' shouted Fifty.

'No. I'll walk with Doodle,' said Jonno. 'Is that OK?' he asked Bee's mum.

'Yes, of course it is. I think Doodle likes you.'

So we left Bee and Jonno with the Beast.

After tea I was about to leave, list in hand, when Little Miss Nuisance came into my room. 'Can I come with you?'

What was Flo asking me that for? Of course she couldn't come with me to the Tribehouse.

'No.'

'Please, Keener.'

'No. In fact, never.'

The conversation carried on for a bit – me saying 'no', and her begging. Most unlike Flo. And she didn't look normal either. She's meant to be pretty, according to people's grannies, but her face was all puffy, like she'd been crying. I didn't care, but I found myself asking her what was wrong anyway.

'What's wrong?'

'I need some help, Keener.'

'Doing what? Has the head come off your dolly again?'

'No. Proper help.'

What's proper help? 'You mean with maths?'

'No. You've got to help Jack, Keener.'

I had no idea who Jack was – one of her cuddly rabbits probably. 'You're going to have to be a bit clearer, Flo.'

'Because of Show and Tell.'

'Flo, there's nothing I can do to make Fat Cat get chosen.'

'It's not to do with Fat Cat,' said Flo, quite crossly – as though I was deaf and she'd been shouting the same thing for five minutes. For someone who was asking for help she wasn't being that polite.

'Fine,' I said. 'If you've got a problem, ask Mum.'

Flo started to cry – big tears. I still didn't care, about Flo, or about Jack, whoever he was. She put her head on my lap (I was sitting down) and started sobbing. I could feel my trousers getting wet. I was desperate for her to stop.

'What do you want me to do, Flo?' I said to the blond hair on the back of her head. The answer was a bit muffled, but I heard the word 'Tribe'.

'Lift your head up and say it again.'

'We need Tribe, Keener. Please let me come with you.'

I found myself nodding. I mean, she is my sister.

'All right. All right. You can come, as long as you're *nice*.'

I wish I could be properly nasty like Copper Pie is to his brother. He'd have said, 'Hop it, Crybaby,' chucked her out of his room and slammed the door.

I told Mum Flo was coming over to Fifty's and she made an I'm-so-proud-of-you face. Amy made an it-can't-be-happening one. As we left the house Flo reached up and took my hand. No way was I walking along like that. I told her to stay by my side.

'What's it all about then?'

'You know we had Show and Tell the day before?'

'Yesterday, Flo. It's called yesterday.'

'Yesterday,' she repeated. 'Yesterday, we had Show and Tell and Jack brought in his motorbike medals.'

'Jack's too young to have a motorbike.'

'He has got one. It's little and he drives it in muddy fields. He had photos.'

'Lucky Jack.' *How unfair was that? A Year 3 with a motorbike.*

'He's not lucky, Keener. Someone took the medals.'

'As a joke?'

'No. For really.'

'For real, Flo.'

'For real, and Jack started crying, and Mr Dukes talked to us and said one of us must know who took them.'

'A thief,' I said. 'That's not good. But what's it got to do with Tribe?'

I stopped at the edge of Craven Road to wait for a gap in the cars. Flo stepped straight into the road.

'Flo!' I grabbed her arm and pulled her back. I may not like her much but I don't want her squished.

'Sorry, Keener.' She took my hand and I let her. The chances of anyone we knew seeing us were pretty slim.

'So go on then. What's it got to do with Tribe?'

The answer was simple. Jack put his medals back in his desk after Show and Tell but they weren't there at the end of the day. Flo wanted us to get them back, somehow . . .

'We're not detectives, you know. And anyway the teachers'll find out what happened.'

Flo started whimpering.

'Is he your friend?' I asked.

She shook her head.

'Well why do you care then?'

'Because it's not nice to take something,' she said.

She's right, I thought, but I didn't say so.

'OK. I'll see what the others say,' I said. The rest of the way I kept Flo happy by talking about other animals Flo could make out of all the pom-poms she'd made. A guinea pig came out top.

Fifty was playing on the floor of the Tribehouse with Probably Rose. He was rolling a ball that made a jingly noise as it turned over and Rose was meant to be rolling it back, but Fifty kept doing it for her. Bit pointless.

'Hi,' said Fifty, followed by, 'Hello Flo. What are you doing here?'

'Can you say, Keener?' she said.

'Flo wants our help,' I said. 'Tribe's help.'

'Doing what? Actually don't answer that.' He disappeared up to the house with Rose, and came back without her.

'Come on then, Flo. You can sit on my seat and tell me what it's all about,' said Fifty, pointing to the safe. (I think Fifty quite likes my sister.) She sat there and told him the story of Jack's stolen medals.

Show and Tell

'I loved Show and Tell. I used to spend all week deciding what to bring. Why don't we have Show and Tell in Year 6, Keener?' said Fifty.

'Because it's boring. Because it's for show-offs, like you. Because no one ever has anything interesting to show. Because the same people got picked *every* time. Because we're past the stage where we want to know about someone's piece of stripy rock from Cornwall, or their pom-pom Fat Cat.'

Flo's lip trembled. I gave her an I'm-a-nice-brother-really smile.

'I'm not though,' said Fifty. 'I'd like to see Fat Cat and I'd like to take my fire steel in to show how to light a fire without matches . . . and there's my indoor sparklers. Everyone would like them.'

'Grow up, Fifty,' I said.

He stuck his tongue out at me and turned to talk to Flo. 'So there's a criminal at work in Year 3, is there?'

Flo nodded.

'And you want us to catch him.'

Flo nodded again.

'OK. Don't see why not. How are we going to do it?'

'How are we going to do what?' said Jonno, walking in, followed by Bee who said, 'And what are you doing here, Flo?'

Flo explained the problem again, with a bit of help from me and Fifty.

'That's really mean,' said Jonno. 'Why would someone steal someone else's medals? It's not like money you can spend —'

'Or sweets you can eat,' said Fifty.

'Of course we'll help, Flo,' said Jonno.

'Help what?' said Copper Pie, the last to arrive. We should learn to wait for all the Tribers before we talk about things. Then we wouldn't have to repeat everything.

'Help find out who took Jack's medals,' said Fifty.

'From his desk,' I added. *Detail might be important.*

'Is Jack the tall one who's always got his sweatshirt on back to front?' Bee asked Flo.

'Yes,' she said.

'He's a headcase,' said Copper Pie. 'He's got a dirt bike. So's his brother. They race them.'

'That's what he got the medals for,' I said.

'So what? Even headcases deserve to have their Show and Tell treasures back, don't they?' said Fifty.

'But how do we get them back?' said Bee.

'Metal detector?' I said.

'Idiot,' said Bee. (She's been saying that a lot lately. Tribe should ban it.) 'It would pick up every bit of money, zips, knives —'

'We'd be doing the school a favour if we found knives,' said Fifty.

'It would pick up fire steels too,' said Bee, glaring at Fifty. He always has his fire-maker in his pocket.

'We could search the school,' said Fifty, ignoring the Bee stare. 'It would be risky to take someone else's medal home. How would you explain that you suddenly got medals for racing a motorbike when you don't even have one? They're probably stuffed behind something.'

'We looked for them at school,' said Flo. 'They weren't in our classroom but they could be somewhere else.'

'Maybe they're down the loo,' said Copper Pie, always ready with a sensible suggestion!

'I know,' said Jonno. 'We could interview everyone in Flo's class, looking for signs that they're lying. That might work.'

'What signs?' I said.

Jonno ran through the seven signs of lying.

THE SEVEN SIGNS OF LYING

1. No eye contact. You look in their eyes but they look away.
2. Stammering. Lots of umms and ahs.
3. Blinking, blushing or fidgeting.
4. Saying things that just don't sound right.
5. Refusing to answer questions, maybe even accusing other people of lying.
6. Letting you change the subject randomly. People telling the truth will ask why you changed the subject.
7. Touching your nose (think Pinocchio).

'OK. What should we ask?' said Fifty.

'Let's work out a set of questions so everyone gets asked

the same thing,' said Bee. She was warming up to the idea of being a detective. So was I. And it seemed a Tribish thing to do – help a Year 3 get back his biking awards. I wondered what they looked like.

'What do they look like?' said Bee, reading my mind again.

'They're on stripy ribbons, red, blue and yellow,' said Flo. 'There are three of them. They're gold on the outside and they have a motorbike on the inside.'

'Well done, Flo,' said Jonno. 'You were obviously paying attention.'

Flo smiled. She was clearly feeling a bit better.

'What shape are they?' I said.

Flo thought for a second. 'I don't know the name.'

'She could draw it,' said Bee. 'Get the paper, Keener.'

I did as I was told. I usually do. Flo drew a circle, with a badly drawn bike in the centre, and a pattern round the edge.

'It's called a circle, Dodo.' *Did my sister not know the basic shapes?*

'I know that, Keener. But it's a circle with lacy bits.'

OK. Whatever.

Flo budged up to make room for me on the safe so I could write out the plan for the interrogation. Flo had a few ideas but they weren't any good so she shut up – I guess she realised we were older, and better.

It took up the whole meeting – no time for my list. But I didn't mind. It was Tribe's first criminal investigation – the mystery of the missing medals.

116

Flo pushes her breakfast round her bowl

I typed the questions we'd agreed, printed a copy to check that it looked all right and made four copies.

INTERROGATION QUESTIONS

1. Did anyone apart from Jack touch the medals?
2. Do you think they're lost, not stolen?
3. Did anyone seem particularly interested in them?
4. Where do you think they might be?
5. What is your favourite dinner?
6. Who do you think might have done it?
7. Have you got anything else to say about Jack's missing medals?

I also did copies of the seven signs of lying so we'd know what to look for. I put it all in my rucksack, together with a list of all the people in Flo's class, which I got off the class email. There were twenty-eight of them, twenty-six excluding Flo and Jack. That meant we had to interrogate five kids each, with one left over.

'We're all set,' I said to Flo at breakfast.

She pushed her Shreddies round and round.

'Why don't you try eating one,' I said.

She ate one. And then pushed the rest round her bowl again.

'What will you do if you no one's lying?' she said.

'No idea,' I said. 'And anyway one person must be lying. The person who took the medals.'

'What are you talking about?' said Amy. She'd made a big pink lipstick mark on her orange juice glass.

'Nothing,' said Flo quickly.

I kept schtum.

'Suit yourselves,' said Amy.

Flo pushed her hardly touched breakfast away from her. I scraped the last speck of cereal off the bottom of my bowl – I don't mind the sound but Amy hates it. I scraped my bowl again, even though it was all gone, and finished my orange juice.

'Bye, Mum,' said Amy. She was off to meet spotty boyfriend. Flo says they snog on the way to school. She saw them on the corner of the alley when Mum drove the back way one day when they were late.

'Can't you just look for the medals, Keener?' said Flo. 'They must be at school somewhere. Fifty said so.'

'But they could be anywhere. And anyway then we wouldn't know who stole them. Unless they were in a desk. Don't worry, Flo, we'll get the guilty kid.'

Mum spotted Flo's full bowl. 'Flo, would you like a banana instead?'

Flo nodded and took a bite from the peeled banana, but as soon as Mum turned her back to us she shoved the rest in her school bag.

That'll be mush, I thought as I left for school.

Fifty was waiting on the corner. It must have been hair wash day in his house because his curly locks were extra extra curly. I didn't say anything. I've learned not to tease him about his bouffant hair. I gave him the sheet of questions and the clues to lying. He had lots of his own questions.

What if the kids won't answer?

How will we make them?

What will we do when we find the guilty one?

'Let's ask the others when we get to school,' I said. It sounded better than 'no idea'.

All the Tribers were already on our patch. Fifty repeated his questions. Jonno gave the answers. 'Flo's class will *want* to help Jack find his medals. Everyone will want the thief caught and the medals returned.'

'They won't,' said Copper Pie. 'I told you, he's a headcase.'

'But even if you don't like someone, or he's a headcase, you still wouldn't want him to lose something that really mattered,' said Bee.

I thought about whether I'd want arch enemy Callum to get something back that he loved. *Nope, I'd rather he stayed miserable.* I kept that thought to myself.

'How are we going to let them know about the interviews?' I asked instead.

'Flo can tell them,' said Bee. She shouted across the playground to where my sister was sitting by herself.

'Is she all right?' asked Fifty, watching her walk over to us. I nodded.

'What?' said Flo.

'Tell your class to come to our patch at break —'

Jonno interrupted. 'That won't work. Too many at once. Flo, tell all the kids with names that begin with A to L—'

Bee took over again. 'First names or last names?'

'First,' said Jonno.

'OK.' Bee paused to make sure we were all concentrating. 'Flo will get all the kids with first names that begin with letters A to L to come here at break for the first round of questions. OK, Flo?'

She nodded but it wasn't a believable nod, if you know what I mean. Bee spotted it too.

'Would you rather I got the kids rounded up?'

Flo nodded, a proper nod this time.

'I'll go and talk to them when they're lining up,' said Bee. In charge as usual.

'Real names or nicknames?'

'Shut up, Keener.' Bee was impatient to sort it all out. 'The rest, with names from M to Z, can come at lunch. So by the end of school we'll know who did it.'

'But what will we do with the guilty one?' I asked.

'We'll tell the Head, of course,' said Bee.

It sounded simple, but I was sure it wouldn't be. *Catching thieves was bound to be more complicated than a sheet of questions and Jonno's lie-detection manual. Wasn't it?*

the kangaroo
court

Yes, it was more complicated than we thought.

At break, about twenty kids from Flo's class tried to squash into our den between the netball court's wire fence and the tree, which was almost all of them. *Trust her class to all have names from the beginning of the alphabet.*

There was pandemonium for a bit until Bee used her foghorn voice to organise them all into five lines, with a Triber in front. My first one was a girl called Izzy. She looked terrified. I looked down at the sheet and read the first question. 'Did anyone apart from Jack touch his medals?'

She answered, 'No.'

I looked down at the other sheet, with the signs of lying. I couldn't judge the first one – no eye contact – because I forgot to look at her. I went on to the second sign – there was no stammering, but then again it would be hard to stammer over a word with only two letters. I scanned the rest to see if

I could work out whether her answer was a lie or the truth. But I realised that I needed to ask more questions, ideally ones that would get her to say more than one word.

'Is that it, Keener?' said the little girl, who had stupid bunches, like dog's ears, hanging either side of her face.

'No, Izzy. There are a few more questions.' I rattled them off, being sure to study her for signs of blushing, fidgeting, loss of eye contact, etc. There were none. I was fairly sure she was not guilty, so I wrote NG by her name. She watched me.

'You can go now,' I said.

She stayed where she was and gave me a sickly smile and I felt my face going the pinky colour. *Yuck, a Year 3 who likes me!* Luckily it was a boy next: George.

George wasn't very cooperative. His answers to the seven questions went like this: don't know, maybe, can't remember, no idea, spaghetti bolognaise, the tooth fairy, no. He walked off. I had another kid waiting but first I needed to decide whether George was G or NG. It was tricky. He was fine on the eye contact and stammering and blushing, but when I asked him his favourite dinner, which we put in to catch the liar out, he was meant to say something like, 'Why do you want to know that?' but he said 'Spaghetti bolognaise'. According to Jonno's list, a person who is telling the truth will ask why there's a random change of subject, but a liar will answer even if the question's completely off the wall. It worked with Izzy. She said, 'I thought this was about the medals, not about dinner?'

'Are you going to ask me anything or not?' said the next in line.

I quickly scribbled NG by George and moved on to Ayesha. She had a lot to say and didn't take any breaths along the way. We'd got as far as 'Who do you think might have done it?' when the bell rang for end of break.

She answered anyway, naming every boy in the class without any gaps. 'GeorgeCharlieDanBenHughJoeShakil . . .'

I skipped the last question which was, 'Have you got anything else to say about Jack's missing medals?' She was a definite NG.

'How many did you interview?' asked Bee.

'Three,' I said.

'One,' said Fifty. Bee gave him an I'm-disappointed face.

'Five,' said Copper Pie, and gave Fifty an I'm-better-than-you face. I gave Copper Pie a how-did-you-manage-that face.

'Three,' said Jonno. 'What about you?'

'Three,' said Bee. 'So that means we've done fifteen.'

'But how many were rotten cheating liars?' said Fifty.

'None.' I shook my head. So did everyone else.

'Well, that's good,' said Bee. 'It means we know the guilty one is one of the last eleven. It'll all be sorted by end of lunch. Tribe does it again.'

We did a mini Tribe handshake and plodded back into class.

'Right class, it's mental maths. You know what to do. Books

out and pencils ready. I'll read the questions and you answer what you can,' said Miss Walsh.

Alice's hand shot up.

'No, Alice. There can't be any questions about this. We do it every week.'

Jamie stood up and shouted out. 'She's dropped her pencil, Miss. It's under Ed's seat.'

'Jamie! You do not shout out, you put your hand up. Haven't we been through this enough times?'

Jamie sat down, said 'Yes' and then put his hand up. Ed picked up Alice's pencil and gave it to Jamie. Callum took it off Jamie and gave it to Alice.

'Right,' said Miss Walsh. 'Are we all ready?'

'Yes,' shouted Jamie, with no hand in the air.

Miss Walsh sighed, retied her bun-type thing and read out the first question.

I try and get top marks so I was concentrating quite hard when the Head came in and interrupted Miss Walsh's flow.

'You know who you are. The five of you, follow me!'

You can tell a lot by the way people speak. The Head was *not* inviting us for tea and scones, if you get my drift.

In the Head's office there are pictures everywhere. Loads were done by the kids in school but some are posh in gold frames, and there is a certificate and a photo of the Head being given a cup and another photo of the Head opening the school library after it was 'modernised'. I liked the library the way it was before, when the books were all over the place in no order and you could take out what you liked. Now there's a system and you have to sign 'out' and back 'in'. (I was having a good look at the walls because I was too scared to look at the Head.)

'Enough is enough,' she said. 'A kangaroo court indeed! What were you thinking?'

There was silence. So Bee spoke. 'What exactly is a kangaroo court?'

'It is a cowboy court.' The Head looked at our faces and gave us another clue. 'A court that cannot possibly deliver a sound judgement because it is made up of people who are not equipped to understand or implement the law. A lawless court. A bogus court. A sham.'

I was getting the picture. The Head had obviously found out about the Year 3 interrogations. And she didn't seem to be impressed, which was odd considering we were trying to catch the thief for her.

'We were only trying to help,' said Jonno. 'Flo, Keener's sister, said that Jack was very upset.'

'She begged us to help,' said Fifty, making a prize-winning begging face together with praying hands.

'What is it about the five of you? I know you to be decent, responsible children, yet you cannot walk around a corner without causing some disruption or other. I have had to talk to you about bribery, about emails sent without authority . . . Can you not follow the basic rules of school, which are not dissimilar from those of life?'

It was a question, but no one had an answer. I smiled, hoping to remind her of the decent, responsible bit before she handed out the punishment.

'You will do no more interrogations of the Year 3 class, and you will personally apologise to those you have already quizzed. Mr Dukes is expecting you. Go away, and do not attempt to interfere further. We, the staff, will address the matter of Jack's medals. Try, for the rest of the term – which is, after all, the end of your time in this school – to think before you act.'

Not bad advice, I thought.

'Yes, we will,' said Bee. 'Thank you.' As I followed Bee out of the door I mumbled a 'thank you' too.

Mr Dukes is Flo's teacher. He's all right. We trooped off in his direction.

'That's so mean,' said Bee. 'We'd have had the case all wrapped up if only she'd let us do M to Z.'

There were murmurs of agreement. Me, I didn't care about Jack. I was happy to be let off. Fifty knocked on the door and we went in.

'A-ha!' said Mr Dukes. 'Here come the NYPD.'

No one laughed except Copper Pie. 'New York Police Department,' he explained. There were a few more giggles. I glanced over at Flo but she didn't look at me. *Perhaps she feels guilty that we've got in trouble because of her,* I thought. We hadn't agreed who was going to say sorry but Jonno spoke first so that was fine. He said all the right things, as usual, except for the last sentence, which was: 'If anyone knows anything about the medals but is too scared to tell a teacher you can tell one of us.'

Mr Dukes didn't like that. 'Children, you don't need to turn to the Year 6s, you can always come and talk to me in private, as I'm sure you know.'

He nodded at us, which meant LEAVE. So we did.

'The mystery of Jack's missing medals will stay exactly that, I reckon,' said Fifty.

'What do you mean?' said Jonno. 'Tribe was appointed by Flo to find out who did it. We're not giving up.'

I should have known.

old-fashioned
detective work

Bee's mum was waiting at the gates again, with Doodle. Bee was about to go with them when Jonno said, 'Do you want to come round to mine?'

'Too right, I do,' said Bee. 'Sorry, Mum. I'm off to Jonno's.'

'But what about Doodle?' said Bee's mum.

'He's your puppy,' said Bee, and walked off.

'Can we *all* come to yours?' said Fifty.

'Yeah,' said Jonno. I was mega-excited because I was the only one who'd ever been inside his house. The others had never seen his fabulous stuff: telly, computer, executive desk . . .

'But won't your dad send us away?' asked Fifty. We all know Jonno's parents don't much like kids.

'No. He's too polite. But he might suggest I don't invite you again, after you've gone of course. That's how it works in our house.' So we went to Jonno's. On the way Fifty made the mistake of asking Bee how the dog was settling in.

'The *dog's* fine,' she said. 'It's me that's not.'

BEE'S REASONS NOT TO HAVE A PUPPY

- They poo randomly. They wee randomly. (At least Bee's brothers used the bathroom, even if they did sometimes wet the seat.)
- You need stair gates everywhere to keep the dog and its mess in the kitchen.
- Bee's puppy has already chewed the leg of the red armchair and eaten one of Bee's mum's boots. Bee's hidden all her stuff.
- Puppies eat grass and then they throw up. Doodle sick went behind the radiator.
- Outside, Doodle acts like a wind-up toy on superfast setting and tramples all over the flowerbeds.
- Doodle hates his crate (he's meant to sleep in it). He has to be shoved in. (Bee's thinking of moving into it instead, to get away from him.)
- Puppies cry like babies. They wake up in the night, like babies.
- Puppies are always hungry (like Bee's brothers).

Bee didn't stop for breath for about ten minutes.

'Where'd your mum get the mutt from anyway?' said Copper Pie.

'Some posh woman Mum works with couldn't cope. She'd only had him for a few weeks. She told Mum and next thing Doodle was ours. She must have been desperate to get rid of him – she gave us *everything* free! But that's not how it's meant to work, is it? You're meant to beg for a pet for years. You're meant to hope every Christmas Eve that there'll be a tiny fluffpot in your stocking. You're NOT meant to have a crazy dog move in with all its rubbish while you're at school one day.'

We walked the rest of the way in silence.

Jonno's dad was busy somewhere else but his mum was in the kitchen, writing. She took out her earphones, smiled at us all, said, 'Hello, I'm Frances. You must be the Tribe.'

We all said our names.

She smiled (again), put her earphones back in and went back to her writing. The beads in her hair made the same clackety-clack I remembered from the first time I met her. I waited for her to say something else, maybe offer us a snack, or at least a drink . . . but she was obviously busy.

'Come on.' Jonno led us all upstairs to his room and I watched the faces of the Tribers as they clocked all his gear.

'You are *so* lucky,' said Bee.

Copper Pie put the telly on and started flicking channels. Fifty swivelled on the see-through plastic computer chair, with his feet dangling because they didn't reach the floor. Bee had her mouth wide open. She didn't seem to know what to do. Jonno did.

'Right, Tribers. Time for a new plan. We can't interrogate the Year 3 bambinos so we'll have to try something else. Ideas?'

Complete silence, except for the commentator yelling from the telly. Copper Pie had found football. Fifty was messing with the web, in between spinning round. Bee didn't seem to have anything to say (odd). I was wishing I'd sat on the computer chair before Fifty so I could play the game I played last time.

The complete absence of anyone saying anything was interrupted by Jonno's mum. She poked her head round the door, nodded towards the telly, raised her eyebrows, smiled, nodded towards Fifty, who was going round quite fast, shook her head, and left with a beady jingle.

'Copper Pie,' said Jonno. No response. He said it again. 'Copper Pie!'

C.P. answered without taking his eyes off the screen, which was about a nose-length from his nose.

'What?'

'Mum doesn't agree with telly, unless it's something she approves of, which means David Attenborough or the news.'

'How come you've got a telly if that's how she feels?' I said.

'To watch DVDs when they want me out of the way,' said Jonno. 'You'd better either turn it off or kill the volume.'

Copper Pie grunted, and muted.

Fifty slowed down. 'Do I need to get off the chair? I don't

think she approves of spinning either.'

'No, don't worry, she can't see through walls, so you're safe, unless she checks again.'

I was beginning to see that maybe Jonno's mum wasn't quite as fantastic as I thought she was. There seemed to be a lot of invisible rules that I was slowly discovering, like secret writing in lemon juice slowly turning brown from the heat of a lamp (you must have tried it!).

Fifty hopped off the seat anyway, landed on two feet, immediately wobbled, nearly fell over, wobbled again and finally grabbed Bee.

'All that spinning has affected your inner ear,' she said.

Fifty let go, stood up, still weaving slightly from side to side, and made an announcement. 'So, Tribe, despite the setback of the kangaroo court, has to find the answer to the mystery of the missing medals. Are we all of the same mind?' He does that occasionally – speaks like someone in a play.

'Yep,' said Jonno.

'Don't mind,' I said. I meant 'No' but that didn't seem the right answer. Copper Pie half turned round, opened his mouth, and then went straight back to stare at the silent telly instead.

'Well, if we don't, it'll seem like Tribe failed . . .' said Bee.

'Same,' said Fifty.

A bit more silence. I remember thinking that after Jonno joined we'd never ever run out of ideas again. Seemed like I was wrong.

'We either need to find the medals, or the thief,' I said. To help things along.

'We could offer a reward,' said Jonno.

'That could work.' Bee pulled the pocket of her jacket out. 'But we don't have enough money.' Bee never has any money.

'Maybe we could get chatting to the ones in Flo's class we didn't interview and see what we find out.' A useless suggestion from Fifty, but at least he was trying.

Bee spoke in a very slow you're-an-idiot voice. 'The Head'll *never* guess what we're up to if we start hanging out with Year 3s. Duh!'

'What's your idea then ... *boss*?' Fifty was getting his own back.

Bee sighed. 'We could get Flo to do it for us.'

'Right,' I said. 'Flo, who never stops talking, likes pink and babies, is going to conduct police interviews with the (twenty-six kids take away the fifteen we've already grilled) eleven kids we didn't get round to? Don't think so,' I said. 'She'd ask the questions *and* answer them.'

'She'd make them swear on her dolly's life,' said some sound waves from somewhere near the telly. Copper Pie was watching football *and* listening to Tribe. I don't think any of us thought he was that clever.

'I don't think finding the thief is going to be that easy,' said Jonno. 'We should concentrate on trying to find the medals.'

'Same,' said Fifty.

'But how?' I asked.

'Old-fashioned detective work,' said Fifty. 'Also known as searching thoroughly. I mean, do you really think the Year 3s looked properly? We could take sticks to poke down the radiators, and a feather duster to swish out anything under the cupboards and on the high-up shelves.'

Copper Pie turned round, all the way this time, and said, 'Waste of time. They're probably in the bin,' before turning back to the football.

Bee had had enough. She marched over to the telly and turned it off. 'Last time I looked you were a Triber, like us. How about helping rather than shouting out rubbish, in between watching mindless morons try and put a ball in a net so big even *I* could score?'

WOW! I wasn't sure how Copper Pie was going to react. She'd insulted him, and worse, his great love – footie.

'OK,' said Copper Pie, standing up and looking down at Bee's ponytail. 'I can see you need help.' (Ha ha.) 'Let's spread a rumour that we're gonna uncover the thief in the playground at lunch.'

'And . . .?'

'And, if it was me, I'd come and confess and beg you not to tell the whole school as long as I give back the medals.'

'Top idea,' said Jonno. 'Football's obviously good brain juice.'

I was stunned. Since when did my old friend, Tribe's trusty thug, have ideas like that?

Copper Pie gave Bee a wide smile. She wanted to be

miffed, I think, but she couldn't help grinning back. 'I like it,' she said.

'So how do we spread the rumour?' said Fifty.

'That's easy,' I said. 'We tell Flo.'

'Tell her what?' said Fifty.

'Tell her that we've found out who stole the medals and we're going to announce it at lunch. She'll be full of it. How Tribe discovered —'

'So we lie to Flo?' said Bee.

'Well, we can't tell her the truth – that it's all a hoax. She'd let it slip. She has to believe it's true if we expect her to blab to everyone.' I didn't mind lying to Flo. It was in a good cause, after all.

Bee looked at each of us, checking. 'OK.' She shrugged. 'It's a plan. We tell Flo it's all solved and we're identifying the culprit at lunchtime.' She slapped her hand down and we did a Tribe handshake.

'Flo'll be really excited that we've solved the crime,' said Fifty. 'She was so upset about it, wasn't she, Keener?'

I nodded, despite the fact that we hadn't *actually* solved the crime yet. Fifty seemed to have forgotten that.

'Will *you* tell Flo?' said Bee.

I had a quick think. If I told Flo that we knew who had stolen the medals she would go on and on and on at me until I broke, like a tortured prisoner of war, and told her everything.

'Why don't you?' I said.

'Fine,' said Bee. 'I'll tell her before the register.'

'Sorted,' said Jonno. He walked towards the door. 'It's probably time you were off.' We'd only been at his for about twenty minutes! I hadn't played on his computer. We hadn't had a snack. We hadn't done anything. I looked at him. He looked kind of weird. 'I'll ask Mum if you can come another time. She doesn't really like having a lot of kids in the house when she's studying.'

It was the first time I'd ever felt sorry for Jonno. Usually I want to *be* him.

The four of us trudged down the stairs. Jonno came to the door with us.

'Are your friends leaving?' came his mum's voice from the kitchen.

'Yes,' shouted Jonno.

His mum came into the hall. 'Bye, everyone.' She smiled. I didn't smile back. Jonno's mum was a bit of a mystery herself. All nice on the outside, but . . .

'See you tomorrow,' I said to Jonno, and I made a fist. We banged knuckles in a fist of friendship. He shut the door and we headed up the road.

'What was that all about?' said Fifty.

'If I didn't know Jonno better, I'd say he was scared of his mum,' said Bee.

'No, that's me,' said Copper Pie. 'My mum's the scary one.'

'Your mum's not scary. She just shouts a lot,' I said.

'Same,' said Fifty. 'It's my mum who's the scary one. Always trying to have cosy chats so she *understands* me. I don't want to be *understood*. I want to be fed sugar.'

'At least your mum doesn't cry,' said Bee. 'That's scary.'

Seemed like I was the only one with a normal (ish) mum. I decided I'd better join in anyway. 'What's scary,' I said, 'is having a mum who sends you to school dosed up on a deadly combination of pink, white and yellow medicine and wrapped in a vest, even though you're only a whisper away from falling into a coma.' I liked the way they all shut up and listened. 'A mum who thinks nothing of sending you out in all weathers with a throat that makes swallowing as painful as eating a . . . hedgehog.' (Wished I'd picked a better scratchy thing.)

'Does she really make you wear a vest?' said Fifty. I didn't answer. I didn't need to. They laughed all the way to where I turn off. I wished I'd shut up.

a friday
feeling

'What are you going to do next, Keener?' said Flo at breakfast on Friday morning.

'Nothing,' I said.

'But you promised to help.'

'We tried,' I said. 'But the Head won't let us carry on with the interrogations, so that's it.'

'Can't you do something else?' she said.

'Nope.' I wasn't going to mention anything about the hoax planned for lunchtime. That was Bee's job.

'Can't you look for the medals at school? They might be behind the radiator, or by the coats.'

'They're not likely to be though are they?' I said. She's quite thick, my sister. People think she's bright but they've got her wrong. 'Who would steal something from your classroom and then hide it near where they took it from?'

'Please,' she said.

I was getting fed up with the medals business. 'Why do you care about Jack's medals if you don't like him?'

Flo, the sister who always has something to say, the sister who is little but has a big mouth, said nothing. Her mouth made a few shapes that suggested something might come out, but no sound followed. I had a revolting thought. *Maybe she's in love with Jack. Maybe she wants to find the medals so she can give them back to him.*

'I never said I don't like him,' said Flo and burst into tears, which brought Mum. I got a version of the usual being-kind-to-your-sister lecture. Blah blah. It made no difference to me. I am me. Flo is Flo. We will never be friends. I couldn't remember why I'd tried to help her in the first place. I grabbed my bag and left.

Fifty and I caught up with Copper Pie, who was kicking a stone to school.

'You're early,' he said. He's usually first.

'Keener had to escape from the evil eye of his evil sister,' said Fifty.

'You wait,' I said. 'One day soon Probably Rose will turn round and say she hates you.' As soon as I'd said it I knew it was a mistake. Fifty's face lost all its bones and went all soggy. I wished I could take it back.

'But she won't mean it, because she's really . . . great.' I was going to say nice or kind but they didn't sound good enough. Anyway, it worked, because Fifty gave me a I'm-so-glad-you-like-her-too look (and Copper Pie gave me a sideways you're-a-weirdo look) and we carried on to school.

Jonno was talking to Bee on our patch. They stopped when we got there.

Copper Pie clapped his hands together. 'All set to catch the thief?'

'We just need Flo,' said Bee. (She doesn't get to school until about half-past eight.) While we waited, Fifty, Copper Pie and I peeled the bark off our tree and compared shapes. If you're careful you can get great big bits. I managed to get Italy (a long boot) and a duck. Fifty cheated and made an F. Copper Pie made a shotgun and pretended to shoot me. *Remind me, why is he my friend?*

'Can't you stop doing that?' said Jonno. 'Loads of creatures live under the bark.'

It's no fun having your own Tribe entomologist.

'She's here anyway,' said Fifty, pointing at my sister.

'Off I go then.' Bee flicked her black fringe out of the way – it falls straight back over her eyes but at least she gets to see for a second.

We watched Bee walk across the playground, avoid being hit by an out-of-control diabolo and miss a stray netball chucked by a Year 5 (who *must* need glasses) doing goal practice. Bee tapped Flo on the shoulder and she swivelled round. I couldn't hear what was said but I knew as soon as Bee left she'd be off, spreading the news.

Bee didn't come straight back. She went over and spoke to

Ed and Lily. I watched Flo to see how quickly she'd work her way round the Year 3s. Except she didn't move. She stayed where she was.

A funny feeling started growing inside. A sort of have-we-done-it-all-wrong-again? feeling. I don't know why, because either the thief would confess, or he wouldn't. What could be simpler? I tried to push the worry away and replace it with one of Dad's 'Friday feelings'. Fridays are great because the weekend starts, and Dad comes home early. He says that all day he has a holiday feeling. A holiday feeling sounded good to me.

'Did she believe you? asked Jonno, when Bee finally made it back, thirty seconds before the bell.

'I think so. But she didn't look too happy about it. She said it would be kinder if we whispered in the robber's ear. She said it was mean to tell the whole school.'

She's right, I thought.

'What did you say to that, Bee?' I asked.

'I couldn't agree, could I? So I said we were doing it because the thief needed to learn a lesson.'

The have-we-done-it-all-wrong-again? feeling rose up again, smothering the Friday feeling. It was going to go wrong. I just knew it.

the rest of
friday

This is what happened.

ABSOLUTELY

NOTHING

All through break I waited for some Year 3 to come up, all tearful, maybe with a friend, and confess to the crime. All through lunch I kept scanning the hall to spot the kid, red-eyed and head bent over, coming to find us – Tribe, the rooters-out of evil. But no one came. No one even looked a bit dodgy. In fact the only dodgy-looking people were the Tribers, who were all on high alert waiting for the medal-nicker. Afternoon break followed the same pattern. Except that Flo came over to our area.

'Have you done it?' she said. 'Have you said who's the thief?'

I looked at Bee. It was her lie. So she needed to sort it out.

'No, Flo. We . . . we might have made a mistake.'

She'd put all her faith in Tribe, but we'd failed. I knew she'd be disappointed. *Please don't start sobbing again,* I thought.

But all she said was, 'Oh.'

'Sorry, Flo,' said Fifty. 'But we'll keep trying, won't we?'

Jonno nodded. His woolly hair bobbed up and down. I looked at the floor. The medals were turning into a pain in the neck. We were never going to get to the bottom of it.

a change
of venue

It's not a rule or anything but lately we've started meeting at the Tribehouse on Saturday afternoons as well as Wednesdays. When I arrived, Jonno was there already.

'Hi.'

'Hi.'

The Tribe flap flapped and Bee arrived. Copper Pie came next.

'Mum gave me some biscuits.' He plonked them on the safe.

'Why?' said Bee.

'Because the nursery kids didn't like them.'

'They must be bad then,' said Bee. 'I'll pass.'

'Suit yourself.' Copper Pie took one – it was a biscuit sandwich with a layer of chocolate in the middle. I took one too.

'Lush. How could anyone not like these?' I said, reaching for a second.

'Mum said that one of the children said it looked like nappy mess.'

I nearly gagged, but managed to tell my brain that I *was* eating chocolate spread, nothing worse.

Fifty shot in as though he'd been thrown out of a cannon. He'd smelt sugar, for sure.

'Excellent,' he said, eating one and holding a second ready for immediate digestion. He *loves* sweet things. Unfortunately his mum doesn't *love him* having sweet things. She says they're mostly full of artificial sweeteners that will make today's children really ill with lots of horrible diseases (whose names I can't remember) when they're older.

'Right,' said Jonno. 'Fist of friendship.'

We did the fist thing, a bit stickier than normal thanks to the biccies. I'd got the list I made on Wednesday with stuff for Tribe to do, and I was about to get it out but Jonno spoke first. He's done that to me so many times. I'm going to have to work out a way to get in before him or I'll spend my life never saying what I want to.

'I know we failed yesterday, but I feel like Tribe made a pledge to Flo to clear up the medal business. Surely we can think of something between us.' He looked at us all in turn.

We couldn't exactly say 'no' – it just wasn't Tribish.

'OK,' I said. 'But I haven't got a clue what to do.'

'All right,' said Copper Pie.

'Same,' said Fifty.

Bee made an I'll-go-along-with-the-rest-of-you face.

'Come on then.' Jonno headed out of the door.

Where's he going? I thought.

'Where's he going?' said Copper Pie.

'Search me,' said Fifty.

'Come on,' said a disembodied voice from the garden, so we did what he said.

'Where are we going, Jonno?' Bee asked the back of Jonno's fluffy head.

'Keener's.'

'Why?' said Bee.

'Because that's where our only lead is.'

Bee turned round to look at me. 'Why are we going to yours?'

I shrugged. 'Ask him?'

'Jonno, why —'

He was already through the cat flap so Bee didn't bother with the end of her sentence. We all wriggled through after him.

'We're going to Keener's because we need Flo. She was there. She's our best witness.'

Great! We were going to spend *all afternoon* getting nowhere with Flo. I was miffed, so I hung back, hoping someone would notice. But no one did so I caught up. No one noticed that either. Jonno and Bee were talking about Doodle – they sounded like parents! Jonno seemed to know a lot about dogs, considering he doesn't have one.

'How do you know so much about dogs?' asked Bee.

'My friend, Ravi, the one from Glasgow. He had a Labrador called Taylor,' said Jonno. 'She looked a bit like Doodle, but not as curly.' That explained it.

Copper Pie was telling Fifty how he managed to get through five interviews with the Year 3s so quickly. 'I gave them twenty seconds to answer. If they didn't say anything – too bad! How come you only did one?'

Fifty made a smug kind of smile. 'I wanted to be absolutely sure the kid wasn't hiding anything so I asked all the questions and then asked them again in a slightly different way. Cunning of me, don't you think?'

I thought about joining in – explaining how I did my interrogations – but I was in a mood. And knowing we were on our way to see Flo didn't make it any better. She was bound to be all bossy when she realised Jonno *needed* her.

'I didn't expect you back so soon,' said Mum. 'Or there to be so many of you. Has the Tribehouse fallen down?' (Her idea of a joke.)

'No,' I said. 'We've come to —' It occurred to me just before I said the next word that Mum might not agree with us being on the trail of stolen medals.

'We've come to play with Keener's models,' said Fifty.

'That's right,' I said and walked past Mum, out of the door and up the stairs. I could hear Flo upstairs. She was talking to her cuddly toys. 'Don't cry, there are a few bumps and then you'll be at the bottom.' She was obviously mattress surfing again. She likes to warn the toys so they don't get scared. Mum says it's role-playing. I think it's stupid.

We waited on the landing for her to slide down from the top floor. Whoosh! She nearly ran into Jonno who was standing right by the bottom stair.

'Hello Flo,' he said.

'Hello Jonno.' She smiled. 'Have you got another idea? Shall we look in all the classrooms on Monday? Maybe behind the radiators? Or by the coats.' Flo sounded really happy, for the first time in ages.

'No. I've got a better idea, but it needs you.'

'Me?'

'Yes. We need you to sit down and go through every single thing that happened in Show and Tell. Where everyone was sitting? Where Jack showed off his medals? Who went before him? Who went after him?'

Flo's face switched from happy to terrified.

'It's all right, Flo,' said Bee. 'It's to get ideas, isn't it, Jonno?'

'Partly. But also because if you go through it step-by-step you might remember something that you didn't before. The police do it all the time. It's called a reconstruction.'

Flo started sobbing. 'I don't want to do it, Keener.'

'Yes you do – you love talking,' I said. That didn't exactly help. She pushed past me and went into her room. She tried to slam the door but there was a cuddly toy in the way (exact species unknown: a cross between a bear and a dog) so there was no 'slam', only a decapitation (just joking).

Bee knocked on the slightly open door. 'Flo,' she whispered.

'Go away,' said my angry little sister.

'Come on,' said Fifty. 'Let's play with Keener's Deathmobile.' (I didn't use to like anyone messing with my models but we're Tribe now and sharing is part of it.)

Fifty bagsied my hammock. The rest of us found things to shoot him with as he swayed. Copper Pie had his own catapult, of course, I grabbed the Deathmobile (which shoots missiles), Jonno had a rocket that launches foam darts but Bee was empty-handed.

'I'll have this,' she said. 'Whatever it is.' She hoicked a long blue handle out from behind my skimboard.

I laughed. 'It's not a weapon.'

'It is now,' she said, swinging my metal detector round like a ball and chain.

'Cool,' said Jonno. 'Does it work?'

'Not very well,' I said. 'Dad buried some money in the sand for me to find when we were on one of our trips. Even though he knew exactly where he'd put it we never found the 50p.'

Bee turned it on. It made a long beep.

'That means it's alive,' I said.

'What does it do when you find metal?'

'It makes little bleeps with gaps in between and the closer you get, the smaller the gap between the bleeps.'

Bee wanted to metal detect my room but we wanted to

fire stuff at Fifty.

'OK. I'll try somewhere else.'

Off she went.

In between launching attacks on each other we talked about you-know-what.

'Who would bother to steal someone's medals?' said Fifty. 'You'd have to find a way to take them with no one seeing you. Then you'd have to find somewhere to hide them. It would be silly to take them home because your mum would know you haven't been out winning competitions on the dirt bike *you don't have* without her knowing. All too much trouble.'

'You'd have to be really mean,' said Jonno. 'And a bit stupid because there's a risk you'd get caught. There are easier ways to get back at someone.'

'Hitting them works,' said Copper Pie. We all laughed. He stood up and pretended to box. Fifty slid out of the hammock and boxed as well. I didn't join in. The trouble with pretend fighting is that Copper Pie sometimes forgets the 'pretend' part. Jonno hasn't worked that out yet. He stood up and got a karate kick in the chest. It must have hurt but he didn't say anything. He took his glasses off and put them on my bookshelf, did a few shoulder rolls (to limber up) and launched himself across the room, screaming something that sounded Chinese. Copper Pie sidestepped and then the three of them rolled around on my rug for ages as though they were about four years old. I reclaimed my hammock and watched them being idiots. It would have gone on and on if Bee hadn't come back in with my red-eyed sister and told them to stop.

'Flo's got something to say.'

It took us a few seconds to get the right way up and the right way round.

'Go on then,' I said.

My sister's hand, which was behind her back, crept round to the front. She was holding something. *Another terrible pom-pom animal most likely*, I thought. I got ready to say how lovely her pom-pom guinea pig was . . . but I was wrong. She was holding three medals. They caught the light as they swung gently from side to side on their stripy ribbons.

Flo is the
thief

No one spoke. It was too awful. I wanted to throttle her. My sister, a thief! She started sobbing. Good. *Sob all you like,* I thought. *You're in dead trouble.*

'Flo, you need to stop crying and tell them why you've got Jack's medals,' said Bee.

'Because she took them,' I said.

'Leave it, Keener,' said Bee. Charming! My sister steals precious medals and I get the grief.

'Come on, Flo.' Bee's voice was kind, not like her normal bossy one.

'I took them.' She started to howl.

'Shh,' said Bee. 'Do you want your mum to hear?'

What did it matter? I thought. Everyone was going to know soon – Mum, Mr Dukes, the Head.

Flo wiped her snotty nose on her sleeve, and the tears slowed down. 'Sorry,' said Flo.

'Don't worry, Flo,' said Fifty.

What!

'Why are you being so nice?' I said.

'There must be an explanation,' said Jonno, looking directly at me.

'Let's hear it then.' I was all ears. I folded my arms and stared at Flo, evil-personified. She gulped, looked up at me, looked quickly back down and started talking in a very small un-Flo-like voice.

'Jack was really mean.' Big sniff. 'He said Fat Cat was dead because she hasn't got legs. He said they'd been chopped off by the Fat Cat butcher.' *OK. Quite mean. But not bad enough to steal from Jack's desk.* 'And then he said Fat Cat was ugly, even uglier than me.' Another big sniff.

'But Flo, you can't take things from people because they upset you,' said Jonno.

'I wasn't going to keep them. I was going to put them back.'

'So why didn't you?' I said.

'I was too scared. I didn't want to get found out.' She started crying again.

I sighed. Fifty was nearly in tears too. He's so soppy about girls.

'Hang on there, Flo,' said Jonno. 'Something doesn't make sense. Why did you ask us to find them if you knew where they were?'

'I was too frightened to put them back in Jack's desk. I thought if I put them in the muddle by the coats and bags and lunch boxes, the bit Mr Dukes is always telling us to tidy, *you* could find them and *you* could give them back. But you wouldn't do it.'

'So that's why you kept asking us to look for them at school,' I said. It was all fitting together. Flo wanted *us* to agree to search the school. Then she was going to put the medals there for *us* to find, to keep *her* out of trouble. Not a bad plan. Perhaps she wasn't that dim.

Flo nodded. 'If you'd done what I'd said Jack would have them back already and you wouldn't be cross with me.' A big tear rolled all the way down her cheek.

'We didn't do what you said because if the medals were by the coats they'd have been found already.' I was cross, but not as much as before. She did look totally pathetic, all wet-faced and blotchy. And Jack *was* wrong – she's not as ugly as Fat Cat. No one's as ugly as Fat Cat.

'So where were the medals?' asked Jonno.

'In her pom-pom box,' said Bee. 'With Fat Cat.'

'And where's that?'

'In her toy cupboard.'

'How did you find them, Bee?'

'By using the metal detector that doesn't work very well.' She held it up. 'I was messing about, trying to cheer her up, and the bleeps starting getting closer together. So I followed them. And hey presto, there were the medals.'

I gave Flo a disappointed look.

'I wanted to tell you,' she said.

'If you'd wanted to tell us, why didn't you? I said.

'Because she was embarrassed. And that's why she wouldn't do the reconstruction, isn't it Flo?' Jonno peered over his glasses at her.

'I didn't want to lie anymore,' she said.

'So, what are we going to do about Flo?' said Bee, hands on hips.

'Nothing,' said Copper Pie.

'We've got to do something. We need to return the medals to Jack, *without* being caught.' Bee raised her eyebrows. They disappeared under her fringe.

'Is that what we're going to do?' I said. 'Do you think that's fair? Fair and TRIBISH?' I shouted the last word.

'Well, she's sorry. Aren't you, Flo?' Flo nodded at Bee.

'So if you're sorry about something, that's enough, you cry and everyone covers up for you?' Ten eyes turned to me in horror.

'Well, we can't turn her in,' said Copper Pie. 'I wouldn't even do that to Charlie . . . I don't think.'

'Great! So we can steal cars, laptops, phones . . . and as long as we're sorry, it's OK.'

'Keener, listen. You can see how bad she feels. It was a mistake. If we hand the medals in, saying we found them by the bags, like Flo planned. Problem solved. Jack gets his Show and Tell back. Flo will never do anything like it again.'

'Please, Keener. Please.' Flo tried the big-eyes look. It almost worked.

'I bet we've all done *something* we're ashamed of,' said Fifty. 'Something we'd rather forget.' I didn't like the way he was looking at me.

THINGS TRIBERS ARE ASHAMED OF (DON'T TELL ANYONE)

COPPER PIE: When Charlie was a baby Copper Pie used to feed him his mashed up food, but he ate most of it himself, so Charlie didn't grow very much and cried a lot because he was hungry. It stopped when Charlie learnt to speak and told his mum.

BEE: Used to drop her sweet wrappers when her mum wasn't looking, but one day a man ran after her and told her off. (She'd never do that now - she's eco.)

FIFTY: Pretended to be four (when he was actually nine) so he could go in the Soft Play with Probably Rose, but accidentally went too fast down the slide and took out three toddlers.

JONNO: Told his mum he'd lost his expensive denim jacket, but really he put it in a bin because he didn't like it.

KEENER: Went to feed the ducks with Fifty but the geese started trying to get the bread, so Keener threw the bag at Fifty and ran away, leaving his friend to be pecked to death.

'Come on, Keener,' said Jonno. 'She's your sister.'

'And what if Jack was your brother?' I said. 'And he'd been crying at home about his lost medals. How would you feel then?'

There was silence. I'd made a good point – I could tell.

'We'd feel differently,' said Bee, eventually. 'But we're not Jack's friends or family, we're Flo's. It's about loyalty, Keener, something Tribers are meant to know all about. Come on, Flo. Let's go and mattress surf and leave your brother to work out what's right.'

Bee took Flo's hand, which seemed very little, and led her out. One by one the others followed and left me on my own, with the medals lying on my blue rug.

Mr Dukes

'Mr Dukes,' said Bee. Mr Dukes bent his head slightly to show he was listening. (He really is quite a nice teacher.) 'We found these.' Bee held out her hand and the three coloured ribbons slipped over her fingers, making the medals dangle down and bang each other.

'Excellent,' he said. 'Jack will be pleased. Where were they?'

'Under where the coats are,' said Fifty. 'We decided to search the school really well in case the medals were lost, rather than taken. We started by the Year 3 classes and there they were!'

'Strange,' said Mr Dukes. 'We searched thoroughly ourselves.'

'Not thoroughly enough,' said Bee, with a cheeky little smile that made me want to puke, but made Mr Dukes smile.

'Well, thank you very much.' He disappeared back into the classroom. We disappeared back to our patch for the rest of break. Job done.

MR DUKES'S CLASSROOM – 11.01 A.M.

Mr Dukes: Jack, good news. Some Year 6s found your medals.

Jack: Brilliant. Where did they find them?

Mr Dukes: Outside the classroom, amongst all the debris.

Jack: We looked there.

Mr Dukes: You can't have looked well enough.

Jack: But we did.

Mr Dukes: Well perhaps the Year 6s are better at looking.

Jack: Who was it who found them, Mr Dukes?

Mr Dukes: It was Bee —

Jack: And the Tribers. I'm right, aren't I?

Mr Dukes: Good guessing. Yes, it was. You might want to thank them.

Jack: I'll go now.

Mr Dukes: Not now, Jack. Break's over. You can find them at lunchtime.

Jack: If I was a Triber *I'd* have found the medals.

Mr Dukes: I don't think being a Triber had anything to do with it.

Jack: It did, Mr Dukes. They can do anything.

Mr Dukes: They're ordinary children, like you, Jack.

Jack: No, they're not. They're . . . different.

Mr Dukes: Sit down now, Jack. And keep hold of those medals.

the ballerina's head

At lunch, Jack came to see us on our patch. It was totally embarrassing. He thanked us five hundred times and wouldn't go away. It felt so fake, pretending we were heroes when in fact we were accomplices of Flo the thief. He asked loads of questions about Tribe that we tried not to answer. (And he had his sweatshirt on back to front – always does according to Bee.) Eventually he got bored, and went off to muck about with his cronies.

'We *so* don't need Jack thinking we're his best friends,' said Bee.

'I agree,' I said. 'I mean, if he hadn't been mean to Flo she wouldn't have been mean back.'

'If that's what you think, how come it took you a whole weekend to decide whether or not to cover up for Flo?' Fifty asked me. *Good question.* But I had the answer.

'It didn't,' I said. 'I decided right away. But I wanted to

make sure she was properly sorry so I made her wait.'

'You're evil,' said Copper Pie, but he was laughing. Bee and Jonno weren't. I could see they thought I was a monster.

'Don't look at me like that,' I said. 'I told her last night. After I'd made her do all the vegetables for Sunday lunch, and the washing up, and the drying. Amy tried to help but I explained that Flo had been nasty and she wanted to make it up to me by working hard. I waited until Mum had put her to bed and then told her I'd decided to go along with the plan to return the medals. Simple.' *(No way was I ever going to tell on Flo. Far too risky. She'd be poisoning my blackcurrant and cutting holes in the bum of my trousers forever more.)*

'Keener, you are one mean brother,' said Bee.

'No, I'm not. Flo's one mean sister. And if you're interested, what I spent most of the weekend doing was investigating how it was that my metal detector could find three little medals in a box of woolly pom-poms when it couldn't spot a 50p buried in sand even when it was right over it.'

AN INVESTIGATION BY KEENER INTO MY RANDOM METAL DETECTOR

I collected ten different things, all of which were metal or had metal in them. I tested them to see which ones made the machine bleep. I also measured the distances between the plate of the metal detector and the object, at the point the bleeping started. I even buried some of the objects in a plant pot full of mud and tested that.

THE OBJECTS
Key, nail clippers, beer-bottle top, spinning top with metal middle and rubbery outside, baking tray, Flo's scooter, a pin, another pin but with a green plastic end, fork, red plastic magnet.

CONCLUSION
My metal detector is completely random. It bleeps when it feels like it. Finding the medals was luck.

'Who cares. We found the medals. That's all that counts,' said Bee. 'Let's forget it. I mean Show and Tell is really Show Off and Tell. Do you remember that pottery ballerina that Annabel Ellis brought in and said she'd *made*?'

'How *could* we forget?' said Fifty. 'You nearly broke the ballerina's head off trying to wrestle it out of Annabel's hands to see if it had a *Made in England* stamp on the bottom.'

'Which it did,' said Bee. 'And I remember being desperate the next week to find something amazing to take in to *really* annoy her.'

'That's what *we* should do,' said Jonno.

'What?' said Bee.

'We should help Flo find something amazing to take for Show and Tell. Something Mr Dukes would be interested in. It would make her feel good. And show Jack that she's not afraid to try again, even though he was mean about Fat Cat.' We were all silent. 'What do you think?' he said.

'Let's do it,' said Bee.

'Same,' said Fifty.

'I'm in,' said Copper Pie.

There was only me left. I hadn't decided what I thought so I had to do the thinking bit out loud, because they were all waiting for me.

'Part of me doesn't see why we should help Flo, because *she* was the one who did the stealing. But another bit of me thinks Jack didn't have to be so horrible about Fat Cat – even though it's rubbish. And the other thing is, Flo never gets picked. You know what teachers are like. They always pick the same kids.'

'They pick kids like you, Keener,' said Fifty. *He's right. They do.*

'I think it would be nice if she could be picked just once.'

'That sounds like a yes to me, Keener,' said Jonno. I rewound the scene in my head and listened to what I'd said. Jonno was right. It was a yes. *Show and Tell, here we come,* I thought.

'I know!' I said. 'My swimming medals. They're bigger and shinier than Jack's medals, and there are more of them. And there's a silver cup too. Flo could take them.'

Bee sighed. 'That wouldn't work, would it? They're not hers. *She* didn't win them. You did.'

'But Jack doesn't know that,' I said.

'Keener, for someone who's clever, you're quite thick. Flo needs to take something *she's* proud of. Taking *your* medals would be another lie. How is your little sister meant to work out right from wrong if her big brother can't?'

Good job my mum and dad didn't hear that, I thought.

'Good point,' said Jonno. 'We need Flo. Only she can decide what she's proud of.'

'That won't work,' I said. 'She was *proud* of Fat Cat.'

'We're back where we started then,' said Fifty.

'Exactly right,' said Jonno. He stood up, wiped the bits of bark and general woody stuff off his shorts and disappeared out of our shady patch into the sunny playground. He headed straight for Flo.

show
and tell

Miss Walsh congratulated us in class. She made us all stand at the front. It was even more embarrassing than when Jack did it, knowing we were actually in league with the other side. I went pink, as usual.

'Some of you may know that Jack, in Year 3, lost the medals that he brought in to school last week for Show and Tell. I'm pleased to say Mr Dukes tells me that five members of 6W found the medals by searching the school at break time when they could have been out playing. Children' (she looked at us) 'or should I say "Tribers",' (she winked – how embarrassing!) 'I think it's wonderful that you tried to help, and I'm sure the rest of the class would like to join me in a round of applause.'

There was some unenthusiastic clapping. We sat down as quickly as we could. Being Tribe is great, but everyone knowing we're Tribe is not so great. (It's the attention, I could do without it.) Evaporation, condensation, freezing and melting came next. But Jonno wasn't taking any notice. He spent the whole lesson drawing on a piece of paper stuffed inside his science book. I asked him about it at lunch.

'I'm going to help Flo make Fat Cat better.'

'He's not ill,' I said. (That's about as funny as I get.)

'No, but he's ugly,' said Jonno. He took a piece of folded-up paper out of his pocket and flattened it on the lunch table. It was a drawing with labels showing what each bit was made of. Fat Cat's head and body were still pom-poms, and the ears were still cardboard, but the whiskers were now matchsticks and there were twig legs, buttons for eyes and a tail made of a bit of coat hanger (so it could stick up in the air) with wool wound round it.

'It looks brilliant,' I said. 'But it needs a collar.'

'Good idea.' Jonno drew a collar and wrote *ribbon*, on the label. He held it up so the others could see.

'What's the idea?' said Fifty.

'I told Flo I'd show her how to make Fat Cat even nicer. Good enough to be picked for Show and Tell. This is the plan for her to follow. I want her to make it and tell the class how she did it all on her own. Do you think she'll be able to do it?'

'I'll help her,' I said. (I'm good at modelling. My secret weapon is a glue gun.)

'Not too much, though,' said Bee. 'She needs to do it herself.'

'Tell you what, Keener,' said Jonno. 'I'll give her the plan, but I won't tell her you've seen it. You can accidentally-on-purpose spot her trying to make Fat Cat beautiful and help her if she needs it. OK?'

'Message received and understood,' I said.

'If it's any good, she can make me a pom-pom elephant,' said Copper Pie. He looked deadly serious, so we all wet ourselves laughing. (Quite why he loves elephants I don't know, but he does.) It was one of those great lunchtimes when everything seems funny and we're not bored and we all know exactly what the others are thinking.

Before we dumped the trays and headed out to the playground, Fifty decided to make an announcement. 'Tribers, the mystery of the missing medals has been successfully solved, without anyone being found guilty, which was clever of us. But not only has Tribe forgiven the thief, we are now helping her to see right from wrong, by making delightful toy animals for Show and Tell. Let's hear it for Tribe.'

We did a handshake in the middle of the hall. *Who cares?* Everyone knows we're Tribe.

'I'm off to see Flo,' said Jonno. 'See you later.'

That night I lurked around Flo's room, but I didn't see any evidence of plastic surgery on Fat Cat. She seemed to be playing 'Grown-up Barbies have a Spelling Test'. So I went and got this old book Dad lent me about someone who's nice half the time and evil the other half, bit like Flo, and settled into my hammock. I meant to go and check again after she'd had her bath but I forgot. By the time I thought about it again she was in bed, lights off. I felt guilty. I knew Jonno would be disappointed that Flo hadn't followed his plan. *I'll get up early, there'll be time to do it before school if we bolt breakfast,* I thought.

deluxe
fat cat

Flo was ready for school. Completely ready – dressed, fed, hair combed, teeth cleaned (ish). I hadn't even had my cereal.

'You're ahead of yourself this morning,' said Mum.

'I want to be early. Can we go early, Mum?'

'We might manage it, but I've got a few things to do before we leave, like eat.'

'Can I go with you, Keener?'

My normal response would be 'No', but I thought about it for a second before I said, 'No'.

'I've got something to show you,' she whispered.

'What?' I whispered back.

'It's called Luxury Fat Cat.'

She'd got me interested. I skipped cereal, grabbed a banana and left with Flo.

'Show,' I said as soon as we were out of sight of the house.

'Jonno drew me a picture showing me what to do,' said Flo. 'I like Jonno.'

She reached into her bag and pulled out a plastic wallet. In it there were four sheets of paper all with really careful drawings of pom-pom animals, with labels, just like Jonno had done. The first one was Fat Cat. The rest were Fat Guinea Pig, Fat Elephant and Fat Hippo. All done by Flo.

'They're brilliant,' I said.

'I'm going to make a pom-pom zoo. Do you want to see Luxury Fat Cat?'

'I do,' I said. And I really did.

She pulled out a red velvet bag with a tie-top. (It came with her magic set.)

'Ready?' I nodded. Out came Luxury Fat Cat. And he was excellent. Flo had, somehow, done everything Jonno said, but better. Fat Cat's face (blue button eyes, a sewn-on mouth and nose and plaited grass for whiskers) was brilliant. The fluff of the pom-pom covered all the joins so the legs (she'd used lolly-sticks) and tail looked great as well. And the collar was silver with some writing on it in black. I had a closer look. DELUXE, it said.

'It means luxury in France,' said Flo, beaming at me.

I was impressed. I couldn't wait for the Tribers to see. It was like one of those programmes Mum won't let us watch where they completely change what someone looks like. Fat Cat was now Deluxe Fat Cat. 'How did you do it?' I asked.

'I showed Jonno's drawing to Mr Morris and he gave me

some stuff from the art room. I needed Dad to help' (Mum doesn't do craft) 'so after Mum put me to bed I stayed awake and waited and waited till he came home and then we did it, in my pyjamas, and I didn't go to sleep until it was the day after.'

'Wow!' I was a bit jealous. Dad's never done modelling with me in the dead of night.

Flo and I were second on our patch, after Copper Pie. We waited until all the Tribers had arrived before Flo showed them the drawings, and the 'Deluxe' Fat Cat. Jonno was so pleased you'd have thought she was *his* sister. Copper Pie was over the top about how good it was — I'm pretty sure he wanted to ask for the pom-pom elephant, when she'd made it.

Fifty said, 'You'll blow them away, Flo,' which she liked.

But it was Bee who made all the difference. 'I'm proud of you, Flo,' she said, and gave her a huge hug.

Flo should have been pleased but she started crying again. 'I'm sorry about the medals,' she said. 'I'm sorry I was nasty.' I think she meant it.

'We know,' said Bee. 'And we know you'll never do anything like that again.'

The bell went. I watched Flo join her line and all of a sudden I was worried that after all her hard work Mr Dukes *still* might not let her Show and Tell. Flo turned round to me, winked and waved. In her other hand she had the plastic wallet and the velvet bag, ready for Show and Tell. It was going to be all right. Somehow or other she'd manage to get her turn this time, I was sure of it. I winked back at her.

Thinking about turns made me remember how she got to go in and see Father Christmas twice the time she didn't like the first present he gave her.

FLO AND FATHER CHRISTMAS

Flo came out of the red tent at the shopping centre with a flat present. It was obviously a book. She tore the wrapping off and looked at it with disgust. She was three. 'That's lovely,' said Mum. Flo ignored her and turned to the little girl next to her who'd got a doll with long blond hair and a sparkly silver dress. 'I want that.' The little girl was too shy or nice or whatever to say 'no' so Flo took the doll and shoved the book at her. Mum said, 'Give that back, Flo.' Flo ignored her. 'NOW,' said Mum. Flo threw the doll on the floor and the girl started crying. Mum tried to apologise. Flo marched straight past the elves who were meant to be in charge of the queue, and went back into the tent. By the time me and Mum were in the tent too, Flo was taking another present, not a flat one. She said, 'Thank you very much, Father Christmas,' and smiled her best smile. Inside the present was the doll she wanted. Flo was really pleased. I thought Mum should have told Flo off. But she didn't. So it's not Flo's fault. It's because she hasn't been brought up properly.

And then I thought about how she used to jump up and down when I got home from school and flap her arms because she was so pleased to see me. I might have even liked her then.

Copper Pie gave me one of his friendly punches, the sort that takes five minutes to recover from. I turned round to see the Tribers' faces all smiling back at me. It felt good, solving crimes and sorting out Flo. It felt like, whatever happened, Tribe would always be able to deal with it.

Chicken
Piri-Piri

the mountain
board

Mum was chatting in the playground after school, as usual. She knows all the mums. And all the kids.

'Who's the new boy?' she asked me. As usual Flo answered, even though he's in *my* class.

'He's called Marco and he's —'

'Portuguese,' I managed to say before she did.

'Perhaps we should invite him for tea?' Mum always wants to help people settle in: neighbours, new kids, new people at work . . . That's how we met Jonno. My mum met his mum at the doctor's surgery (Mum *is* the doctor. Jonno's mum was registering as a new patient), and the next thing I knew this strange kid was climbing into our car. It worked out fine (in the end), but I wasn't keen on trying it again. Marco hadn't exactly made a good impression on his first day.

'No can do, Mum,' I said. 'Tribe meeting tonight.'

'He could come the day after,' said Flo.

'It's tomorrow, Flo. And no he can't,' I said, 'because it's Mum's late surgery on Thursday, isn't it? So we'll be with Amy.'

Amy does tea on Thursdays. She's a terrible sister but at least she can cook.

'What about the day after the day after?' said Flo.

No chance! I ignored her, shouted 'Bye', and headed off with the other Tribers, leaving Mum to take Flo home in the car.

There were only four of us, because Bee had rushed off to puppy training class.

'It's about time someone learnt what to do with Doodle,' said Jonno, who was the one who suggested it to Bee in the first place.

'They could mince him,' said Copper Pie, which was not funny. I don't like Doodle either, but the thought of a minced dog made me gag.

'You're sick, Copper Pie,' said Jonno.

It was sunny and we weren't in a hurry to get home so we decided to go via the park (which is code for via the ice cream van).

'I'm having a screwball with as much chocolate sauce as I can put on before the van man snatches it back,' said Fifty. 'Distract him for me, Keener. Get him talking about those kids with the stunt bikes.' The ice cream man hates the stunt bikers!

'I haven't got any money,' said Copper Pie. He never has. We sub him. I've always got money. Mum says I must grow it, but actually it's because Dad gives me his change,

Grandad gives me a tenner whenever he sees me and every Saturday I check all the lockers after swimming to get the pound coins left by people too lazy to pick them up (or too forgetful).

'Two 99s, please.'

Copper Pie held them while I searched for the right money. Out of nowhere came a buzzing whirring noise, like a remote control bee. It got louder and I looked around frantically trying to work out if I was about to be stung or dive-bombed or whatever. C.P. was doing the same. Fifty was clearly deaf because he just carried on troughing. It was like when you hear a siren but you can't tell if it's behind you or in front. I called over to Jonno who was waiting for his orange lolly (weird choice) to see what he thought it was.

'Can you hear —'

I didn't get to finish my sentence. A blur on a mountain board shot across the road and headed straight down the path towards us. He was going about a thousand miles an hour, shouting something like, 'SADAMANAIRA' over and over again. I jumped backwards to get out of the way. Copper Pie tried to do the same but got his foot caught in the strap of the rucksack I'd slung on the ground and fell back through the swing gate that leads into the play area. Luckily he managed to keep the cornets the right way up even though he was flat on his back with the gate clanging against his head.

Copper Pie tried to look up. 'What the —?'

'It's him,' I said, pointing at the shape that was already at the bottom of the slope. 'The new kid.'

Fifty hadn't noticed anything. He was happily licking the rim of the plastic cone the screwball comes in, standing on the grass, exactly where he had been all along. That's what's happens when he gets sugar. Puts him in a coma.

'Amazing,' said Jonno. 'How fast do you think he was going?'

'Too fast,' I said.

'You sound like the traffic police.'

'I was nearly mown down by an out of control vehicle. What do you expect?'

Copper Pie was still on the ground, holding the ice creams in the air. 'Anyone going to help me up?'

Jonno grabbed him under his arms and tilted him to vertical.

'He'd better watch it,' said Copper Pie.

'Who?' said Fifty, recovering from his sugar overload.

'That new boy. He's a marked man.'

road
trip

The puppy training made Bee late for the Tribe meeting. But she didn't miss anything because when she arrived Jonno was *still* going on about how fast Marco went on his board. He was obviously impressed.

'Bee, the new kid was nearly flying on the way home,' said Jonno. 'I've seen Ed go pretty fast on his board but Marco's way better.'

'Marco? said Bee.

I nodded. 'But what Jonno means is that he nearly flattened us.'

'Yeah, Marco's a marked man,' said Copper Pie.

'What are you talking about?' said Bee.

'He was on a mountain board, going like a train,' said Jonno. 'Wish I could do that. He got to the bottom of the slope in the park in a nanosecond.'

'You're not meant to be congratulating him,' I said. 'He's

a lunatic. If he'd hit us we'd have been dog food.'

'Keener, it was only a skateboard, not a tank.' *Thanks Fifty!*

THE INVISIBLE TANK
AN INTERESTING FACT FROM KEENER

It sounds like a stupid joke, or something on a magic show, but it's not. The Army have honestly truly made an invisible tank. It's amazing. There are pictures of it on the internet and a quote from a soldier saying he wouldn't have believed it if he hadn't been there.

They use cameras and projectors to beam images of the landscape on to the tank and it 'disappears'. The soldier looked across the fields and just saw grass and trees – but he was actually staring down the barrel of a tank gun.

That's clever.

'But it didn't sound like a skateboard. It sounded like a . . . a fleet of skateboards at least,' I said.

'Wonder how he learnt to handle a board like that?' said Jonno.

'Who cares?' said Bee.

'Practice,' I said. 'It's all about balance. Your body learns it. The more you do it, the better you are.'

'Says the surf dude.' Fifty made it sound as though I was showing off.

'It's better than being a pyromaniac,' I said.

Fifty immediately got out his fire steel and started making sparks.

'Not in the hut,' said Bee. 'It's made of wood. We'll go up like fireworks.'

'That'll encourage him,' I said. There is only one possible career for Fifty: arsonist.

'I've never been surfing. It looks impossible. How can you stand on a slippy board on water that's moving?' asked Jonno.

'I'll teach you,' I said. Dad's asked me loads of times if I want a friend to come along. 'You can come with me and my dad.'

'You'll have to teach all of us,' said Bee. 'I can't stay at home all the time with Mum following me round the house and stopping for a weep every time she finds something one of the twins left behind.'

'I'll stay with your mum and the mutt,' said Fifty. 'The sea's too cold. And it's for fish and mermaids, not me.'

'Bee's right,' said Jonno. 'We should all go. Would your dad take us?'

'I could ask,' I said. *It might be fun*, I thought. A Tribe road trip.

chicken
piri-piri

It was a completely normal Thursday. We were all sitting in our class listening to Miss Walsh droning on about perimeters and areas. Well, most of us were. Alice was picking a scab on her elbow, and I was trying not to watch, because I don't like blood. Her blood would be preferable to mine, but I'd rather not see any blood at all. Any second it was going to start gushing and then her hand would go up, which is where it is most of the time – asking questions, moaning, needing the loo. Then someone would be sent with her to the nurse to get a plaster and Alice would be happy because a plaster gets you attention. *I should be a psychiatrist*, I thought. *Or do what Fifty's mum does – get paid for making people happier.*

Up flew Roddy's hand. He never puts his hand up, because he doesn't know the answer to anything, doesn't ever have any questions, and generally doesn't need the loo.

'Yes, Roddy?'

'There's a terrible smell, Miss. I feel sick.'

'Try not to think about it,' said Miss Walsh. 'I'll open a window. It is a bit stuffy in here.'

'He's right, there —'

Miss Walsh put the palm of her hand up. It means stop.

'Hand up *before* you speak, please Jamie. We don't have shouting out in the classroom.'

It was a silly thing to say because we *do* have shouting out in our classroom. Jamie had just done it, hadn't he?

'There is a —'

Miss Walsh did the 'stop' thing to Jamie again.

'But I've got my hand up, Miss, so now I can speak, can't I?'

'No, Jamie. You put your hand up and then wait for me to either nod or look at you so you know it's your turn.'

We go through this at least once a week. Jamie can't get the hang of it. Quite why Callum, who is pretty clever, hangs out with dozy Jamie I don't know. Oh yes I do! It's because no one else likes them.

Jamie put his hand down. Alice put her hand up. So did Roddy.

'Please Miss, my arm's bleeding.'

Jamie stood up. 'That's not fair. She spoke and you didn't nod and I still haven't spoked.'

'Spoke-n is the word. And Alice spoke before I nodded because she's bleeding and that's an emergency. Sit down, please.'

People were starting to laugh.

'Mine's an emergency too,' said Jamie, still standing.

Alice's shoulders were wobbling which I think meant she was starting to cry. 'It won't stop, Miss.'

'SHE DID IT AGAIN. SHE SPOKED,' Jamie shouted. Not a good move.

'How dare you raise your voice!' said Miss Walsh in a raised voice. 'Sit.'

He sat.

Out came the tissue box. 'Alice, here, hold this tissue on it for now. You can go and see the nurse at break if it's still bleeding.'

Miss Walsh retied the messy ponytail-bun-thing on the back of her head. She does that when she's in a tizz. Tom's hand went up. He sits next to Roddy.

'We are wasting time here. Please put your hands down unless it's an emergency.'

Tom's and Roddy's hands stayed up. Jamie put his up again. Then so did Alice. It was too much. Copper Pie snorted and let out a huge belly laugh. Bee joined in. I tried to keep a straight face but when I noticed Fifty clutching his tummy and groaning I couldn't keep it in any more. And neither could he. I looked around. Luckily almost everyone else was wetting themselves too. Except for Marco, who was sitting next to Tom and Roddy, looking totally confused. Fair enough. His English isn't bad but it isn't very good either. He probably thought it was stand-up comedy or a

186

lesson in joke-telling. Jonno was doing that shuddery silent laughing, it made his frizzy hair shake, and he was crying so much he'd taken his glasses off!

'SILENCE!'

We tried. It's not easy to shut up when something's that funny.

'Tom. Roddy. What is it?'

'The smell, Miss,' they both said at the same time.

'Told you,' said Jamie. He was heading for trouble. No doubt.

Miss Walsh did a raging bull flare of her nostrils, strode past my row and the one behind, stopped by Roddy and sniffed.

'Right, children. Yes, there is a smell. It's some sort of cooking smell, probably coming from the kitchen. And it's not at all offensive, so put your hands down.'

The hands went down. The giggling trailed off. I looked down at my desk, because if I'd caught the eye of any of the Tribers I'd have been doubled up with laughter again. Miss Walsh tried to go on with the lesson but it was pointless. No one was listening.

The bell went for the end of morning school. She picked up her bag and scarpered. I don't think she should have chosen teaching. It's fine when everyone's behaving properly but if there's even a hint of trouble she's useless.

'Best lesson we've had in ages,' said Fifty.

'Best laugh I've had in ages,' said Jonno. 'What is it with

Jamie? He's like a magnet for trouble.'

'Can you smell anything?' said Bee.

'No,' I said.

The class was nearly empty. Copper Pie started smelling everyone's desks like a bloodhound trying to get the scent of a fox. I thought he was trying to be funny but . . .

'Here it is,' he said.

He stood between where Roddy and Marco sit.

'What?' said Bee.

'The smell. Keep up, Bee.'

She went over. 'So, there's a cooking smell. So what?'

'I know what it is,' said Copper Pie.

'Go on then,' said Fifty.

'Chicken piri-piri. I love it.'

As soon as he said it, I could smell that he was right. I've never tried it but we went to this chicken place for Amy's birthday and the sauce smelled exactly like the smell in our classroom. Before I could say anything, Bee opened Roddy's desk, sniffed it and shut it.

'You're not allowed to do that,' I said.

I got a shut-up-Keener look. She tried Marco's desk next.

'Mystery solved.' She held up a plastic bag. Inside there was a tub but the lid can't have been tight enough because there was a puddle of dark orange sauce with lumpy bits, like sick, in the corner of the bag.

'Chicken piri-piri and rice,' said Copper Pie. 'Told you.'

Chicken Piri-Piri

'KEVOCESTAFAZENDOCOMMAMEMOLCHO?' screamed Marco the marked man with the motorised mountain board and matching motor mouth. *I* jumped a mile. *He* jumped over two desks, snatched the bag off Bee, made a face that could kill a crow (to borrow Copper Pie's dad's expression), ran off and slammed the classroom door behind him. It was all over in a second.

He's going to be the death of me, I thought. We'd had two close shaves in less than twenty-four hours. I decided it might be an idea to stay away from Marco.

'I think we should steer clear of our Portuguese class-mate for a while,' said Fifty, hearing my thoughts again.

'Agreed,' said all the Tribers together.

Unfortunately, someone else decided *exactly* the opposite.

bunking
off

After lunch there was a space where there should have been a body.

'Has anyone seen Marco?' asked Miss Walsh.

I studied the scratches on my desk.

'No, Miss,' said Alice. She had a whacking great bandage on her elbow covering the minuscule scabby bit she'd picked.

'Anyone else?'

There were murmurs: no idea, not seen him.

'Right, could you all get out your extended writing books and carry on with the piece we started on Tuesday. You've all got a beginning so today we're going to try and move the story along by introducing the problem and a decision. Use the planning sheet to remind you. I won't be long.'

Miss Walsh disappeared, like Marco.

'Should we have said about the lunch box?' mouthed Fifty. Good job I can lip read.

I shook my head. Why admit something that might have nothing to do with the reason Marco had vanished? He'd probably gone off on his skateboard to terrorise some old ladies with walking sticks out for their afternoon stroll. Or got lost.

'Same,' he mouthed.

Bee got up and went over to Jonno's desk. They had a quick talk and then she went back and sat down. Jonno winked at me. Amazingly Copper Pie was doing what Miss Walsh said. He was actually writing – if the hieroglyphic symbols he makes can be classified as writing.

If no one else was worried, why should I be? I read the beginning of my story, titled: *The Day of the Great Wave*. We were meant to be writing about a journey – not necessarily on a train or a bus, it could be the sort of journey where you go from being a wimp to being brave, or fat to thin, or thin to fat I suppose – but that would hardly be a happy ending.

I hadn't written one word when Miss Walsh flew back in.

'I'm very pleased to see you all sitting quietly. Carry on working on your own. Hands up please if you need any help.'

Alice's hand shot up. Yawn!

'Where is Marco, Miss?'

'It appears he went home, Alice. I expect he felt unwell and wasn't familiar with the rules, which are . . .?'

'We mustn't leave the school grounds without a letter,' said Alice.

'Excellent. So let's get on, shall we?'

The journey in my story was a second-by-second

description of lying on my surfboard in the green water far out at sea, way beyond where the waves were breaking. I was waiting for the perfect wave. I watched as a massive wave built up until it was like a wall of water behind me. I got ready (positioning my board and getting my head together – after all, surfing's a dangerous sport) and then paddled like crazy to stay ahead of the white water, before catching the wave and riding the surf all the way in.

'Yes, Alice.'

'I'm stuck, Miss.'

Miss Walsh walked over to Alice's desk and they started discussing *Going to Grandma's House on the Train*. It sounded thrilling – buying tickets, eating snacks, and the highlight – doing a puzzle magazine. She needed to spice it up. Glancing out of the window and witnessing a murder at an old not-used-anymore station would do.

'Can you think of something a little more unexpected, Alice?'

Even though she keeps her voice the same, you can tell Miss Walsh would like to put Alice in solitary confinement. If Alice spent a few minutes thinking, instead of always putting her hand up, she'd have ideas like the rest of us.

The door opened.

'Excuse me, Miss Walsh.' *What did the Head want?* 'Once again, I need to talk to five members of your class.' It sounded serious. And I didn't like the use of the word 'five'.

'Help yourself,' said Miss Walsh.

Chicken Piri-Piri

There was no time to wonder what was going on . . .

'Bee, Keener, Copper Pie, Jonno, Fifty. Come with me please.'

My heart started thumping twice as fast and twice as hard. My face went a raspberry colour. My armpits went soggy. The unswallowable lump appeared in my throat.

I heard a whisper. 'Don't cry, Keener.' It was Callum, obviously enjoying the look of terror on my face. I tried to look not-bothered. I couldn't.

I was last so I shut the door behind me and followed the queue of Tribers marching behind the Head. We went into her room. She sat down and left us all standing in a ring opposite her. She stared at each one of us in turn. The silence was killing me. I just wanted to confess, to whatever it was we'd done. *I did it. I did it. Punish me.*

'I have had a most unpleasant conversation with Marco's father.'

She did the CCTV scan of all our faces again, before she went on.

'I understand you have taken it upon yourselves to rifle through his desk, which is a violation of his personal space. Do you know what I mean by that?'

'You mean it's his and it's private,' said Fifty. 'We're very sorry —'

'AND you have removed his lunch and ridiculed it, which could be seen as . . .' The Head paused.

'Racist?' said Fifty.

What was he thinking of? Racist is a worse word than bully.

'I didn't say that, did I?' said the Head. 'But . . . Marco told his father that you were studying his lunch as though it was something odd or funny.'

'It smelt,' said Copper Pie. 'That's all.'

'Loads of kids smelt it in the lesson before lunch,' said Bee. 'We were trying to find out what it was, that's all. To help out. People were nearly sick.' *Lay it on, Bee,* I thought.

'We didn't only look in Marco's desk. We looked in Roddy's too.' Why did Copper Pie think admitting more crimes would help?

'So that proves it wasn't anything to do with Marco. It was to do with the smell,' said Fifty, looking like a smug, but small, lawyer.

'So you would have me believe the incident was not directed at Marco?' The Head could do with a lesson in plain English. It was almost easier to understand Marco.

'It was directed at the *sm-e-ll*,' said Copper Pie, as though the Head was thick.

'And we didn't laugh when we found out what it was,' said Jonno. 'Why would we? I'd always choose something spicy over a ham sandwich.'

'Me too. I love piri-piri,' said Copper Pie.

'We were about to find Marco to tell him his lunch had leaked when he came in and started shouting at us,' said Bee. Not quite true but . . .

The Head's face relaxed and some of the really deep trenches in her forehead smoothed out a bit. *Much less scary.*

'Perhaps there has been an element of misunderstanding. It isn't easy to join a school midway through the term, as Jonno should know, and, as you may remember from when Jozef joined your class, we need to help those whose first language is not English.'

What was she talking about? Joe could always speak English.

'I'd forgotten that, Miss,' said Bee. 'He used to get all muddled up and now he speaks like the rest of us.'

'Better than some of you,' said the Head, nodding towards C.P. 'But back to the matter of the lunch. Amends must be made.'

Most of my problems had gone away. I could swallow, the beating inside my chest wasn't quite so violent and my raspberry face felt more like pale pink – not that I could see it.

Get on with punishment and let me go back to my daydream about the ginormous wave and me on it, I thought.

'I think it would help Marco, and his parents, to feel more comfortable about his start in the school if he were made to feel welcome. And who better to show them that there was no malice intended than you five?'

Bee nodded. Everyone else did too. We didn't want to, that was obvious, but you can't say 'no', can you?

'He will be back in school tomorrow, and I'd like you to take care of him at break times, including lunch, every day for a week, so that he's not left to cope on his own. By then he should have settled in, and your duties will be over, although of course you still have to be *friend-ly.*' The school motto, again! We don't all have to be friends, but we all have to be friend-ly. 'I know I can rely on you.' She clapped her hands and shooed us away.

'I *don't* want to babysit that lunatic,' said Bee, on the way back to class.

'You're the one who went snooping in desks,' said Fifty.

'Only because Copper Pie went smelling.'

'It'll be torture,' I said.

The only Triber who wasn't moaning was Jonno. Bee noticed too.

'You think we're mean, don't you?' she said.

'Yes, I do. I hated being new, but at least I could understand everything that was going on. He's new *and* can't speak very good English. Don't you feel a bit sorry for him?'

Silence.

Jonno and Bee didn't wait for us after school because they were going to the pet shop on the way home to buy treats for Doodle.

'My friend Ravi, who's got the Labrador, says you have to have treats for the puppy with you *all* the time, so that your dog gets a reward every time it's good.' Jonno was like a talking dog manual.

So that left the three of us to moan about babysitting Marco without Jonno making us feel mean.

'What are we going to do with Marco?' I said.

'What can we do with him?' said Fifty. 'He's a total nutter.'

Worse than that – he's a scary nutter, I thought. I kept seeing his angry face when he leapt over the desks. I'd rather babysit Doodle.

'We could talk football,' said Copper Pie. 'Ronaldo's from Portugal.'

'And I suppose we can tell him everything about school,' I said. 'You know – don't go in the far loo because it leaks over your shoes.'

'Don't go to the dinner lady with the black bun because she's mean with the pasta,' said Copper Pie.

'Never be late for PSHE when the Head takes it. If Miss Walsh is messing with her hair it means she's stressy and about to explode. That sort of thing,' said Fifty.

'But it means a whole week not being Tribe, except after school,' I said.

'Well, we can't get out of it,' said Fifty.

'Maybe Bee could bribe some other kids to do it?' said Copper Pie.

'Bad idea. Bribes always mean trouble,' I said.

'Same,' said Fifty.

Moaning doesn't make you feel any better – it makes you feel worse. 'Let's not think about it,' I said. 'Let's think about the surf trip instead.'

Fifty and Copper Pie didn't look too thrilled. Copper Pie

says he can't swim, but I'm sure it's a lie, and Fifty doesn't like the sea because when we're knee-deep he's underwater.

'Come on, it'll be fun.'

'Let me think,' said Fifty. 'Cold, wet, more cold, more wet, salty, cold, wet. Count me out.'

'Fine. Me, Bee and Jonno then. Wimps.'

'Did your dad really say he'd take us?' said Copper Pie.

'Yep! This Sunday. All the Tribers are invited. It'll be great. We're going to Woolacombe.'

'Great for you,' said Fifty. '*You* can do it.'

'Is it hard?' said Copper Pie. *A flicker of interest*, I thought.

'Think of it this way,' I said. 'You have a great big board that floats. No one cares if you ride in on your belly. That's not hard. That's like lying on a bed that moves a bit.'

'OK,' said Copper Pie. 'I'll come.'

'Mum'll call all the Tribers tonight. Even you, Fifty.'

'The answer's still "no".'

But of course it wasn't.

telephone
calls

Fifty's mum said it would be good for him. 'A day out with his mates doing something outdoors-y will do him the world of good.'

Fifty was shouting in the background. Mum said it sounded like, 'No, Mum! No!'

Copper Pie's mum said she'd be glad to have him out of the house.

Bee's mum said it would give her a chance to train the dog to use the newspaper for his toilet and not the floor. How disgusting is that?

Jonno answered the phone himself. 'My mum's out, but I've asked her and she says it's fine. Thank you very much for inviting me.'

It was all set. Sunday: road trip.

making friends with Marco isn't easy

'Hi there,' said Bee.

Marco ignored her.

She smiled anyway, and tried again. 'The Head asked us . . .'
I think she was going to say 'to babysit you' or something like
that, but she paused so Jonno helped out.

'. . . if you'd like to hang out with us?'

'No,' he said. It was the first word he'd said that I'd
understood. And not a great start.

'You can ask us if there's anything you don't understand,'
said Bee.

Marco made his eyes go close together in a frown.

'We're so-rry a-bout your lun-ch,' said Fifty, sounding
out every bit of every word like people do when they're on
holiday somewhere foreign.

'I am sorry,' Marco said. *Great,* I thought. *We're getting
through to him.* But turns out he was only halfway through

his sentence. '. . . to be in England.' *Oh! Not so great.*

Being friend-ly wasn't going too well. But at least Marco's English was better than we thought.

'What's it like where you live?' said Bee. 'Lived, I mean.'

'The sea,' said Marco. They were only two small words but I immediately saw a picture of Marco in my head, all brown-skinned and dark-haired, swimming like a seal. No wonder he didn't fit in to our concrete playground. He belonged on a beach.

'You lived by the sea?' Jonno asked.

He nodded.

'You're a long way from the sea here,' said Fifty. 'But there's always the pool. Keener had his party there.'

There might just have been a chance of getting into a normal conversation, but Copper Pie blew it.

'What d'you think of Ronaldo?'

'I hate football.' His accent made all the words sound familiar but different. I quite liked it.

'How can you hate football when the only thing famous about Portugal is Ronaldo, and *he's* a football player?'

Marco flashed his black eyes at Copper Pie, turned round and walked off.

'Idiot,' said Bee.

'I've been to Portugal,' shouted Jonno, taking a few quick steps to catch up with the boy we were meant to be looking after, not annoying. Marco said something back but I didn't hear what. But the two of them were talking, which was good, so we left them to it.

'Well that went well,' said Bee. 'Copper Pie, you should try for a job as a peacekeeper.'

'I don't think Marco's interested in peace,' said Fifty.

'I don't think he wants to be babysat by us,' I said.

'Same,' said Fifty.

'But it's not up to Marco, is it?' said Bee.

On that Friday morning, a whole week and a bit seemed a long time. At least we had the road trip to look forward to.

'I'm not coming,' said Fifty.

'What's the problem?' I said. 'We won't let you drown.'

'Too right, you won't. Because I won't be there.'

'That's not what your mum said.'

Fifty tried to look as though he didn't like me. It looked more like I'd stolen his rattle.

'Please come,' said Bee. There was a long silence. 'Please' isn't a word Bee says very often.

'All right,' said Fifty. 'But that doesn't mean I'll get in.'

When the bell went, Jonno lined up at the back with Marco. I was pleased he seemed to have found a way to get on with the mountain-boarding maniac. Jonno could babysit Marco for the week. (I can't wait to start babysitting – all that money for watching telly. Amy takes her boyfriend.)

It was all up to Jonno. Problem solved.

TIPS FOR WHEN THE TRIBERS ARE OLD ENOUGH TO BABYSIT
BY AMY

- Never agree to look after anyone younger than two. Too many things can go wrong: crying, pooing, milky burping.
- Make sure the child is already in bed when you arrive. (Be late if necessary.)
- Make sure you can work the telly.
- Take chocolate buttons for emergency use – all toddlers like buttons.
- Don't eat all the snacks left for you. Leave one, to show you're not greedy.
- Say 'Thank you very much when they pay you.

problem
not solved

Jonno did a pretty good job of turning Marco from an alien into a human. We left them to it at break and by lunchtime Marco was sitting at the Tribe table with us having lunch – smiling, talking and generally being a completely different person.

'Have you got any sisters?' asked Fifty.

'Yes. Two.' Marco held up two fingers.

I made a poor-you face. Fifty made the opposite sort of face.

'What are they called?' said Bee.

'Adriana and Teodora.'

'Who's the oldest?' said Fifty.

'Me,' said Marco, grinning as though he'd won something. 'They are *bebês*.'

It turned out one of his sisters was three and the other one was one.

Chicken Piri-Piri

'My big *bebê* sings all the time.' Marco started singing something in gibberish. Everyone looked at our table.

'What does the little one do?' said Fifty, over the racket.

Marco shut up, put his hands together and rested them on one side of his face. 'Sleep.'

It was quite a laugh getting Marco to tell us the Portuguese words for things like knife and fork, fat, ugly and smelly. In the end, even Copper Pie joined in. Don't get the wrong idea, I still didn't particularly want Marco with us every minute of the day, but I reckoned we could cope for a week.

After school we walked home together, the five Tribers, talking about plans for Sunday. Which were about to change.

The phone rang a few minutes after we got back from our Friday night out at the pizza restaurant. Amy's boyfriend came, again. He still hasn't actually said anything to me. And he's not getting rid of those spots. Flo picked it up.

'Hello, who's there?'

The other person must have said something.

'It's Flo here.'

The other person must have said something else.

'I know. You're going surfing, and me and mum and Amy are going to make beady necklaces and go for a cappuccino after.' You'd think my sister was seventeen, not seven.

I realised the call was for me, but Flo wouldn't give me the phone.

'I'll ask Dad,' she said and passed it to him.

'Who is it?' I asked.

She made a foul face.

'Well, hello, Jonno,' said Dad.

Why was Jonno talking to my dad? Weird.

'I don't see why not,' said Dad.

Jonno was obviously confirming the details for the Tribe surf trip. Trust him to ring and check with Dad. He's like a responsible adult.

'Yes, we'll see you then. Bye Jonno.'

Dad turned to me. 'He's very nice, that new friend of yours.'

'He's a Triber, Dad. We're *all* nice.'

Dad winked at me. Flo can't bear anyone else getting any attention so she scrambled on to his lap. Amy was already on her boyfriend's lap. It's gross.

'So there'll be six on Sunday.'

'That's right,' I said. 'Do you think you'll be outsurfed by the five Tribers?'

'No, I can handle you lot. But what about the mystery guest? Has he ever been on a board?'

'Who's the mystery guest?' I could tell it was a joke or a trick, but I didn't get it. That's not unusual – there are lots of things I don't get until someone else explains them to me.

'Jonno said you're looking after some new boy and asked if he can tag along?'

My mouth fell open. I started to dribble because there

was no bottom lip to keep my saliva in.

'Do I presume from your face you didn't know about this?'

'He hates the Portuguese boy, Daddy,' said Flo.

Thank you, Flo. Always ready with a helpful comment.

'I don't hate him. It's just that we've never taken anyone with us before and I wanted it to be just the Tribers.'

I sounded about five. I knew Dad would be *disappointed* by my attitude. Don't you hate the way parents use the word *disappointed*?

'I'm a bit disappointed —' *See!*

Dad went on about how I should be kind to a boy who's arrived in England all the way from Portugal. And how I should have learnt that it's exciting to make new friends. *But just because Jonno turned out to be one of us doesn't mean anyone else would, does it?* I didn't say that to Dad. I didn't say anything. I was too busy being:

1. mad that Jonno hadn't asked me first;
2. mad that Jonno wanted marked-man Marco to come;
3. mad that Dad said 'yes' without asking me;
4. mad that the day was bound to be ruined;
5. just totally, completely, utterly mad.

'Doesn't chicken piri-piri come from Portugal?' said Amy. That made me even more mad. If we hadn't found the chicken piri-piri we wouldn't have got the babysitting job and if we hadn't got the babysitting job, we wouldn't be taking Marco to Woolacombe on Sunday. Would we?

FRIDAY NIGHT

JONNO ON THE PHONE TO RAVI, BEST FRIEND FROM WHEN JONNO WAS AT SCHOOL IN GLASGOW, OWNER OF TAYLOR THE LABRADOR AND ALL-ROUND GOOD GUY

Jonno: Hi Ravi, it's me.

Ravi: Hello Smee.

Jonno: Are you ever going to get bored with saying that? I said 'It's me', not 'It's Smee'.

Ravi: Don't get your knickers in a twist. It's a joke.

Jonno: But it's a bad joke. And a really old joke.

Ravi: What d'you want? I'm killing the last of the Gweeshans and I need to concentrate.

Jonno: Doesn't matter. Go and kill your Gweeshans.

Ravi: No, go on, spill. I can kill them with one hand.

Jonno: I think I've upset Tribe.

Ravi: You think or you know?

Jonno: I know.

Ravi: What've you done?

Jonno: Invited an outsider in, basically.

Ravi: Is that allowed? I thought no one could join and no one could leave.

Jonno: You thought right. But I didn't mean to do it.

Chicken Piri-Piri

The outsider, Marco, didn't get what I was saying. I told him we were Tribe and now he thinks he's one too.

Ravi: That's easy – tell him he's not. Got to go. The Gweeshans are rioting.

Jonno: But he's coming surfing with us —

Ravi: Knock him unconscious and when he wakes up, pretend to know nothing about a Tribe. That'll work. Byeeee!

a Tribe of
five

I rang Fifty straight after my swimming lesson on Saturday morning (I found eight pound coins left in the lockers which is a record – six pounds was the next best).

'Have you heard about Marco?' I said. Fifty had. Jonno had told Bee, and she'd come straight round to Fifty's with the news. And it was worse than I thought. Marco wasn't only coming surfing with us, Jonno'd actually asked him to *join* Tribe.

Copper Pie was going round after football so I threw my towel and trunks in the general direction of the washing machine and legged it over there as well. Or tried to.

'Bye Dad. Off to Fifty's.'

'Hang on a minute. The boy that's coming with us tomorrow – I think I should call his mum. I don't feel right taking him off for the day having never met the parents, or the boy, in fact.'

'OK.'

'So do you have a number?'

'Nope, sorry.'

'Could you get the number?' Dad raised his eyebrows, which meant 'try and be helpful'.

'I'll text you.'

Dad raised his eyebrows even higher, which meant 'you'll forget'.

'I won't forget,' I said. And legged it, properly this time.

They were in the Tribehouse – Fifty on the safe, as usual, Copper Pie leaning against the wall and Bee standing with her hands on her hips – it means business.

'He can't be a member of Tribe. We're a Tribe of five – that's it. No question. The Tribe waiting list is closed, forever.' Bee was impressive. And it was exactly what I wanted to hear.

'But how do we tell him?' said Fifty. 'We're meant to be babysitting him. We can't tell him to get lost or the Head'll be on our backs again.'

Jonno barged in, out of breath and with steamed-up glasses.

'Sorry everyone,' he said.

I should think so too, I thought.

'I should think so too,' said Fifty. Stealing my thoughts again. 'Going around inviting strangers to be Tribers.'

'That's not fair,' said Jonno. 'Did Bee tell you *exactly* what happened?'

There was some shrugging.

'Well, no one told me,' I said.

'Good, because that means I get another chance to explain,' said Jonno, pushing his mad hair off his face. I don't know why he does that because every single hair springs straight back to where it started. 'Marco *completely* misunderstood me. I couldn't think of much to talk about, so I started telling him that we're Tribe and he thought the "we" meant him too. But I didn't realise at first. I thought he was getting muddled up between "you" and "us" but when I said "we", as in Tribe, were going surfing he got really excited and assumed he was coming too. That's when I worked out he thought he was a Triber too. I tried to put him right but he made that angry face and did some Portuguese shouting so I . . . gave up.'

'Why did you tell him about Tribe?' said Fifty. 'Why didn't you talk about . . . ?'

'The weather?' I said. That's what we're famous for in this country.

Copper Pie wasn't happy either. 'Babysitting doesn't mean blabbing.'

'He's a stranger and he usually speaks Portuguese. What was there to chat about?' Jonno was getting it in the neck and he didn't like it. His voice wasn't apologetic any more. It was miffed. He stared at Copper Pie. 'What would you have done?'

It was a pointless question. Copper Pie wouldn't have tried to be friendly in the first place.

'OK. OK,' said Bee. 'But I bet you made Tribe sound really fantastic, didn't you?'

'I might have,' said Jonno, squirming a bit.

'How fantastic?' I asked.

'I can guess,' said Fifty. 'Initiations, tackling gangs, standing up to the Head in assembly – that sort of thing.'

Jonno nodded. 'That's about it.'

I could see the others thought it made things worse, but I could see a way to use what Jonno had said to put Marco off.

'Maybe,' I said, 'we should make Tribe sound so dangerous, so wild, so . . . scary, that he's too chicken to join. That could work.'

I looked round at the faces of my friends. Copper Pie smiled – an evil smile.

'I like it.'

'Same,' said Fifty.

'Superb idea, Keener,' said Bee. 'What d'you think, Jonno?'

'I'll do whatever I have to.'

'Good,' said Fifty.

'Marco can't be a Triber,' I said. 'He might be all right. But so are Ed and Lily and they don't get to join. I don't want to be nasty but —'

'We get the idea, Keener,' said Bee.

'So, what's the plan?' said Fifty. 'We go surfing tomorrow and spend all day putting him off with tales of how fabulously daring we are? Like the Three Musketeers.'

He pretended to swipe Copper Pie with an imaginary sword. It was hard, because he's so small and cute-looking, to imagine he could be part of a Tribe too frightening to belong to. *Oh well!*

'It won't be that easy to do with Keener's dad's there,' said Bee.

Good point, I thought.

'But the longer we let him think he's one of us, the harder it'll be to shake him off,' said Fifty.

'So let's do it now,' said Copper Pie.

'He's not here, duh!' said Bee.

'But we could get him here, duh!' said Copper Pie. 'Jonno's his best buddy – he could ring him.'

'I could . . .' Jonno looked around to see whether it was a 'go' or 'no go' decision.

'Do it,' said Bee. 'If we get rid of him today, he won't come with us tomorrow, will he?' She clapped her hands together as though it was all sorted.

Jonno got his phone out and made the call.

'He's coming.'

It was almost too easy. We waited in the Tribehouse. I hoped the others had some ideas for scary stories because I had none, zilch, zero.

I had a question though. 'Jonno, why did you ask my dad if Marco could come? Why didn't you ask me?'

'Keener, think about it. Do you think I would ring you or your dad?'

Me, I thought. 'Me,' I said.

'So do you think I asked Flo for you or your dad?'

Me, I thought. 'Me,' I said.

'Exactly. It was Flo who decided to give me to your dad.'

'Figures,' I said. It made me feel better, knowing Jonno didn't go behind my back on purpose, but not better enough to stop worrying about what we could say to scare off Marked-man-maniac-mountain-boarder Marco. We were quiet for a bit. We heard the doorbell. And then we were quiet for a bit longer, waiting for the doorbell-ringer to arrive in the hut, but it can't have been Marco who did the ringing, because no one came.

Except it *was* Marco, and the reason he was so long was because he was chatting to Fifty's mum.

'Hello Tribers,' she said as she came to the door holding Probably Rose's hand. 'I understand there's one more of you now.' She gave Marco a terrific smile and he gave her one back. *Help!*

'Hi,' said Jonno.

'*Olá!*' said Marco, beaming at us all.

'I'll leave you to it then.' Fifty's mum disappeared back up to the house.

'You're just in time, Marco,' said Fifty. 'We've got some trouble and we need muscle.'

Trust Fifty to try and sound like some thug from the underworld. 'Muscle' wasn't likely to be a word Marco knew. We needed to use normal ones.

'*Que?*' said Marco. That means 'what?' Bee used to say it – no idea why.

'Trouble,' said Copper Pie. 'Fight.' He put his fists up to demonstrate.

That worked better. Or did it?

Marco stepped back and put his fists up. Fifty quickly waved his hands about and did the talking-to-foreigners voice. 'No. No. Not with us.'

The fists went down.

'With bad guys,' said Bee.

'And weapons,' added Copper Pie. This time the demo consisted of cocking an imaginary gun, aiming through an imaginary sniper scope, and firing, complete with recoil. There really is no hope for that boy.

'Why fight?' said Marco. He was already looking a bit worried. Time for me to join in.

'Because other tribes have been threatening us.' I made a serious face.

'With voodoo,' said Copper Pie.

'Idiot,' said Bee, under her breath. 'We fight, Marco, because we own this area.' She drew a massive circle with her arm. 'Understand?'

He nodded.

'And if you want to join us, you must lead the battle,' said Fifty. He was really enjoying it – you could tell.

'Go in front,' said Bee. 'On your own.'

'At midnight,' said Fifty. 'Twelve o'clock. Dark time.'

He'd clearly forgotten how to say 'night'.

'With a hood. A black hood.' Copper Pie was trying not to grin as he spoke. 'And a weapon.' He did the cock, target, fire, recoil thing again.

It was all going really well, except I was beginning to feel a bit scared. All alone at night in a black hood with a weapon is the stuff of nightmares. Marco looked round at the five of us. We all stared back.

Jonno, who'd been really quiet, stepped into the middle and adjusted his glasses so he could see over the top of them.

'Will you, Marco, lead the fight for Tribe?'

Marco's eyes were massive and maybe a bit watery.

'No! NO! NO!'

'Then you can't join us,' said Bee, shaking her head and pretending to be sad. 'We will have to fight alone.'

'You,' said Copper Pie, pointing at Marco's T-shirt. 'Not Tribe.' I think he wanted to make it crystal clear.

'Me. Not Tribe,' Marco repeated.

I felt loads of different things at the same time: sorry for Marco, but pleased that he was scared, guilty because we'd been mean, but relieved that it was over. He'd got the message, for sure.

'Let's go and see if Mum'll let us have some biscuits,' said Fifty, all cheerily.

We piled off after him, with Marco at the back. He didn't seem so keen on us now he knew we were warriors of the street. Excellent plan of mine. Probably Rose was already tucking in to a snack. I think it was raisins and apple but she'd obviously spat some of it out so there was a slimy look to it.

'That looks yummy, Rose,' said Bee.

'A-pull.'

'That's right – apple.'

Rose stuck out her tongue to show Bee. Hideous. Fifty did the proud-parent face.

'Can we have something, Mum?'

Fifty's mum pointed at the worktop – there was a bowl of fruit. Fifty made a face. Fifty's mum smiled, opened the cupboard door and brought out some rice cakes. Great! I don't know why she buys them. I don't know why we eat them. They're like cardboard with air holes. Bee tried to give Rose one but she pushed it away and found a soggy raisin instead.

'So what have you done with your new recruit?' said Fifty's mum.

What had we done with our new recruit? He wasn't anywhere obvious. Bee put her head out of the back door.

'Errr . . . he . . .' Fifty was struggling for words. An unusual sight.

'He had to go,' said Jonno.

Fifty's mum is not stupid, not where people are concerned anyway. She knew something was up. *Time for a quick exit,* I thought.

218

'Thanks for the rice cake. Got to go. See you tomorrow, Fifty.'

'What time does the torture start?'

'We'll be here to pick you up at seven-thirty. Don't forget your trunks.'

'I've got a feeling you'll get me in the water whether I've got trunks or not, you mer-freak.'

'Bye Rose.' I was off. Feeling much better than when I arrived. The Marco problem was solved. All I had to think about was paddling out on my board, waiting for *the* wave and having the ride of my life.

(I was quite looking forward to having an audience too. Everyone likes showing off something they're good at, don't they?)

a sticky situation and not from surf wax

Me and Dad were in the car. We had bacon sarnies in our tummies, two boards on the roof and two wetsuits in the boot. We went to Fifty's first, then Bee's, Copper Pie's and lastly Jonno's.

'One more stop and we're off,' said Dad.

'Why? Do we need diesel?' I said.

'No, we're full,' said Dad. 'But we need Marco, don't we?'

No we don't, I thought. We'd forgotten to tell Dad he didn't want to come any more.

'I don't think he's coming,' said Fifty, in an utterly unconvincing voice.

'I think he is,' said Dad, suspiciously. 'I spoke to his dad yesterday. No thanks to you.' Dad looked at me. I'd forgotten all about the text I was meant to send. 'Took me a while to go through the parents on the class list but eventually I found someone who knew the family.'

I was in the front seat, and I wished I wasn't. I also wished someone would say something. No one did. Dad drew up outside an ordinary-looking house and as I didn't jump out to ring the bell, he did.

I turned round to eyeball the Tribers. Trouble. Dad obviously thought we were trying to leave Marco out. What he didn't realise was that Marco wanted to be left out.

The conversation at the door went on for a long time. I couldn't see who Dad was talking to because the porch was casting a shadow. A couple of times Dad turned round and pointed towards the car. It was excruciating not knowing what was going on. Eventually, Dad shook hands with the hand of the person and came back to the car . . . with Marco and what had to be Marco's board in a flash board bag. *So he's a surfer,* I thought.

'You! In the back.' Dad pointed at me. Cross wasn't the word. He was livid. I got out and climbed in the spare seat in the middle row. Marco took my seat. Dad turned round to look at us.

'We are all going to have a nice day. But before we have a nice day, we're going to have a chat. And then there'll be some apologies. So enjoy the ride, Tribers, but before we get in the sea, we'll run through the conversation you had with Marco yesterday. I'm most interested to hear the details. And after that I'll tell you how hard I had to work to make Marco's dad believe you five are not the most evil children that ever lived.'

Dad talked to Marco all the way to Woolacombe. We were

silent, except for a few whispers. I don't know how the others felt, but I felt ashamed. And frightened. My dad hardly ever gets angry. And he never shouts even if he is. I'd rather he did. The calm way he deals with things makes it worse. I wanted it to be over and done with. If I'd had the choice I'd have bent over and had twenty strokes of the cane (like Roald Dahl got from the Headmaster) in preference to two hours waiting for a telling off.

We parked. The sea was looking good. Plenty of nice straight rollers breaking one after the other. Dad got out and we all followed.

'First things first,' said Dad and headed for the beach café.

At the food counter Jonno tried to give Dad a note, I think it was a tenner. 'This is towards the wetsuit and everything.'

'Thank you, Jonno, but you can keep it,' said Dad. He turned to the rest of us. 'I've said I'll catch up with all your parents in the week. They were all so keen to get you off their hands they were offering me money left, right and centre.'

'Err . . . thanks,' said Jonno.

We had more bacon sarnies (Bee asked if they were organic!) and hot chocolate. Jonno sat next to Marco.

'Can you surf?'

Marco nodded.

'I can't.'

'Nor me,' said Bee.

'Same,' said Fifty.

'I can't swim,' said Copper Pie.

Dad nearly choked on his coffee. 'You must be able to.'

'Don't worry, I can float.'

Bee laughed. It was the first normal thing that had happened since we'd picked up Marco.

'So, who's going to fill me in on the meeting you had yesterday in the Tribehouse? The meeting where you told a pack of lies.'

Not me. Especially not with Marco listening.

'I will,' said Jonno. 'I sort of started it.'

That's the amazing thing about Jonno – he's brave. Not brave like a knight charging at the enemy, but brave at facing up to things.

'Go on,' said Dad.

Jonno explained how he was chatting to Marco and accidentally made him think he could be a Triber, but he can't, because no one can join – that's the rule.

'So we had to put him off,' said Jonno. He looked over at Marco. 'Sorry.' Marco smiled as though everything was fine. That's when Jonno ran out of words. So Bee stepped in and finished it off, in a less than honest way.

'We thought it was kinder to let *Marco* decide not to join Tribe, than for us to say he couldn't. We thought if Tribe seemed dangerous he wouldn't want to be part of it.'

Dad didn't seem to see it the way we did. 'So you invented a gang war? And told him he had to lead the Tribe . . . at midnight? Frightening him half to death with talk of weapons.'

Dad looked straight at Copper Pie.

'It might seem mean,' said Bee, not giving up as usual, 'but we were worried about what to do, because we'd already upset him over the piri-piri.'

It must have been because we were so tense, because it wasn't *that* funny, but Fifty and Copper Pie started laughing. Dad had no idea why – you could tell from his face.

'What's piri-piri got to do with anything?' he said, which started Bee off.

Marco stood up, clapped his hands together twice and shouted, '*Now* I understand. No fight.' He said it again. 'No fight'. And clapped again. 'Ha!'

That made us all laugh. Marco had obviously been trying to work out what was going on ever since he stepped in the car, or maybe ever since Dad arrived on his doorstep and dragged him away from his family. I think he'd only just realised that the fight was made-up!

'I'm glad you understand,' said Dad in a giving-up voice. 'I'm not sure I do, but what I do understand is that it's low tide so this is a perfect moment to get in that water, and get barrelling.'

I wasn't sure whether Tribe had got away with it, or whether there'd be more chat later, but I was with Dad. The water looked epic.

strong plunging waves, with shifting beach breaks

Have I mentioned that my dad's a pretty organised guy? Well, he is. On the beach there was Steve, awesome surfer, waiting to give the others a lesson on the basics.

'I thought there were too many beginners for me to deal with,' said Dad. *Great!* That meant me and Dad —

'Come on, Marco. The wind's offshore. The waves are pumping,' said Dad.

— and Marco, could go and play straight away.

Marco had a nice board. I was quite keen to see how he handled it. I think Dad was too. We didn't have to wait long. He ran in, paddled out beyond the breakers and wow! It was like seeing him storm past us on his mountain board except this time he was on fibreglass with no wheels. Carving, stepping, cuttys – you name it, he did it. And he knew which wave to pick every time. He was ripping. So solid you'd have thought the board was velcroed on. Having Marco as a friend didn't seem such a bad idea after I'd seen him stoked. He could do tricks that I'd only ever seen on the big screen.

Dad and I were doing well too, but compared to Marco we were kooks. In fact, I had some major wipe-outs because I was watching him. I saw Dad bail-out doing the same.

KEENER'S SURF TALK

kooks – beginners

offshore wind – wind blowing off the shore (the best)

stoked – very happy

wipe-out – falling off

bail-out – abandoning the board before you get wiped-out

barrel/tube – a hollow wave

soup – the whitewater from a broken wave

sponger – a soft board for kooks

pumping – non-stop good waves

ripping – surfing really well

carving – turning on a wave

cutty / cutback – using the rails to turn back towards the whitewater

rails – side edges of your board

We had two hours of bliss and then it was time to get the others from the Surf Nursery. Only I called it that – and only I found it funny.

'Are you saying we're babies?' said Fifty. He was lying on the beach on his board – it was a tiny yellow sponger. (Keeps kooks from knocking themselves, or other people, unconscious when they mess up.)

'Yep,' I said.

'Even babies would be better than me.'

Steve, the instructor, lifted up the end of Fifty's board and he slid off. 'That's because it's hard to catch a wave if you won't go in water deeper than your knee.'

I laughed. Fifty had obviously stayed in the shallows. *Drip!*

'Remember, Keener, surfing's the *only* thing you're good at,' said Bee.

'And you're someone else who could be good,' said Steve.

Bee beamed. She loves being good at things.

'Did you stand up?' I asked.

'Too right,' she said.

'And then she fell in straight away,' said Fifty.

Bee stuck her tongue out.

'What about you, Copper Pie?' I asked.

'Nope.'

'Nope what?'

'Didn't stand up.'

'But he gets the award for the fastest approach to land

227

on his belly,' said Steve. C.P. had clearly been using his surf-board as a lilo.

'I wasn't going to risk being chucked off,' he said.

I looked around. 'Where's Jonno?'

Steve pointed at someone out at sea. We could see him paddling – one, two, three strokes. He pushed down with both arms at exactly the right moment and the wave carried the board forwards. He put one knee on the deck, slightly lost balance, but only for a sec, and then got a foot planted. The second foot followed and he was up, but he stayed low, crouching over using his arms to steady himself, all the time moving forwards with the wave. At last, he was ready. He stood up, legs working to keep true on the board, and rode all the way in to the shore. We clapped. Jonno (who looked very odd without his glasses) picked up his board, put it under his arm like a pro, snapped off his leash (the lead you velcro round your ankle so that you and the board stay together), and came to join us.

'Good stuff,' said Dad.

I'd never seen Jonno look quite so pleased. *Who'd have thought he'd make a surfer?*

'Well done, dude. I could see you weren't going to give in until you'd cracked it.' Steve shook Jonno's hand, and then headed off to teach his next group. 'Bye guys.'

I was ready for more.

'Who's coming back in?'

Copper Pie and Fifty decided to muck about on the

sand, building a hole. Kids! But Bee and Jonno were up for it.

'Why don't you buddy Bee?' Dad said to me. He meant keep an eye on her. You should always have a partner in the water checking you're on top, breathing, not underneath, drowning.

'I help Jonno,' said Marco.

'Are you sure?' said Dad.

Marco nodded.

I don't know where the time went after that. Bee and I got on our feet together a few times. And I saw Marco and Jonno do the same. Dad stayed out deep. At some point my tummy started to tell me we needed fuel.

'We need lunch.'

'We do.' Bee agreed. We rode in lying on our boards and went to the café, dragging Fifty and Copper Pie away from their fairy castle complete with moat and cannon. I thought the others would come too but Marco, Jonno and Dad stayed in the water. We ordered, said Dad would settle up later, and watched them from the balcony while we ate sausage sarnies (them) and bacon (me). (There is no law against three bacon sarnies in one day.)

'Jonno's got the bug,' I said. It's funny how some people surf for the first time and become madly, crazily, obsessed immediately and others have a good time, but are quite happy to get out.

We'd had hot chocolate, cookies and Copper Pie had

demolished a sausage roll as well by the time they finally got out. I shouted down to them. 'What kept you?'

Jonno did a thumbs-up, and then carried on talking to Marco, like they were best friends. It was so weird thinking that he was the nutter who ran us down by the ice cream van. He didn't seem crazy any more. In fact, he was rapidly becoming a legend. I'd already decided I was going to invite him surfing next time, so he could teach me some of his moves. I felt a little rush of excitement. I could imagine me and Marco, both with our surf hair, mine blond, his black, talking about stuff. I've never had a friend who surfed, only Dad.

The journey home was quiet – all of us cream-crackered. I slept the whole way.

We dropped Marco off first.

'Thank you,' he said. 'No fight. I join Tribe. Thank you.'

I went from dozy to red alert in a nanosecond. He could surf with me anytime, but be a Triber, no. The answer was still NO.

boring, boring, boring

I didn't go to school on Monday because I had a sore throat, again. Mum says if I keep getting them I'll have to have them removed – my tonsils, that is. I wish she wasn't my doctor. She treats all ill people as though they're making it up. I only get to stay home if I can't swallow – she feeds me lumpy food to check. One day I'll choke and then she'll be sorry. Dad worked from home as Mum had a packed surgery followed by a baby clinic.

I swung in my hammock, read, drank squash through a straw and rearranged my model army, about fifteen times. In between I tried to think of ways to block Marco from joining us.

Bee rang to see how I was but spent the whole conversation moaning first about her mum, who hasn't forgiven her dad for making her brothers move out, and then about Doodle.

'Puppy training doesn't work if your mum carries on

doing all the wrong things. If she doesn't stop cuddling him and letting him sit on the sofa, he's never going to realise he's a dog and not a human. It's like he's a baby. And if he doesn't get the hang of the newspaper loo soon, I'm going to go and live with the twins. I haven't met the actress yet – it's so cool that they're living with a star. I bet she's —'

I didn't want to know about the twins' landlady, I wanted to know what was going on with Marco, but I didn't get a chance to ask. Bee rang off. (Turns out Doodle was eating her baseball boot.) I got more out of Fifty.

'I've had an idea, Keener. We need to try to get Marco to make some other friends. That way he won't want to be with us.' *Not bad, Fifty.*

But less out of Copper Pie. 'I haven't talked to Marco. He can't join. No one can.'

I went back to school on Tuesday morning, even though I'd probably have failed the 'swallow' test, because I needed to know what was going on.

'Keener, you're back,' Jonno said, as me and Fifty walked into our patch, or scrubby bit of dirt, whichever you prefer. Bee and Copper Pie were there too.

They filled me in on the events of Monday. It was the usual rubbish: Alice had been told to stop putting her hand up all the time, Callum's idiot friend, Jamie, had been told to put his hand up before he speaks, and Marco'd been told to ask if he didn't understand something so Miss Walsh could look it up in her English–Portuguese dictionary (but evi-

dently she gave up and used sign language), and the Head
had agreed that Amir would take over Earth Day from Bee
when we leave Year 6. I wanted to talk about the 'Marco
problem' but the bell went. And at break, Marco *and* Ed
were hanging around us, so no chance. And at lunch all the
Tribers and Marco queued up together.

'Such a great day on Sunday,' I said when we finally sat
down with our jacket potatoes (me and Bee) and sloppy
pasta (the rest). Now that we weren't dressed in our black
wetsuits I couldn't think of much else to say to Marco. And
we'd lost interest in getting him to say the Portuguese words
for our English ones.

'Thank you,' he said, and carried on eating.

Jonno asked him about school in Portugal and told some
stories about the schools he'd been to. I didn't say a word.
On the way out to the playground I felt totally miffed. I just
wanted to get on with being Tribe. Without Marco.

'Hey, Marco,' shouted Ed. 'Over here.' Off went Marco.
At last! We all trooped to the smelly, damp hole we call ours.

'Let's talk about the problem,' I said.

'OK,' said Jonno. 'What problem?'

I hesitated. *Wasn't it obvious?* 'Marco wanting to be a
Triber, of course.'

'That needs an official meeting,' said Fifty. He put on a
pompous voice. 'I officially call a Tribe meeting. Fists please.'

We did the fist of friendship.

'So who thinks what?' said Bee.

'Nothing's changed,' said Fifty. 'He can't join.'

'What about you, Copper Pie?' said Bee.

'What do you think? I nearly lost an ice cream thanks to him, remember.'

Two votes against. I decided to speak. 'He's not one of us. It's not the same when he's about. He can't be a Triber.'

'Over to you then, Jonno.'

'He's cool. And he's different. I like him.' *What?* 'But he's not a Triber.' *Phew!*

'OK,' said Bee, flicking the famous fringe so she could give us the stare. 'I agree. So how do we get rid of him, nicely, Tribishly.'

'We should tell him the rule that we decided at the beginning: no one can leave and no one can join,' I said.

'Off you go then, Keener,' said Jonno.

Fair point. It was easy to say it behind his back, but not so easy to say to Marco's face.

'What about your idea, Fifty?'

Fifty looked at me as though he didn't remember ever having an idea.

'About getting Marco to make other friends.'

'Oh, that,' said Fifty. 'I gave up. Couldn't think of anyone he'd like.'

'How can you be so clever and so stupid at the same time,' said Bee. 'We make Marco hook up with Ed. It's perfect.'

'Why is it?' said Jonno. I'm glad it wasn't just me who was confused.

'Because Ed has a mountain board, and so does Marco. Because Ed is always in the park, and so is Marco. Because Ed is so much more like Marco, outdoor-sy and cool, than any of us are.'

I could see what she meant. It was hard to imagine Marco sitting in the Tribehouse listening to us giggling about the water tray in Reception class when he could be zooming down the hill in the park, almost killing unsuspecting members of the public. It was even harder to picture Marco hanging around under the trees with us, watching all the other kids (like Ed) in the playground playing dodgeball, kneeball, football, or made-up-ball.

'So how do we do it?' said Fifty.

There was one of those depressing gaps in the conversation where you hope someone has the answer but no one does.

'It's risky – but I've got a kind of idea. But it's a bit like the other idea we had that got us in trouble,' said Jonno.

It didn't sound too hopeful. 'Go on then,' said Bee.

Jonno sighed and ran his fingers through his springy hair. 'We invite him to the meeting tomorrow, not to join, just to see how it goes.' *Where was this going? Sounded dangerous to me.* 'And we invite Ed too.' *Interesting.* 'And we have a boring meeting – really boring.'

I butted in. 'And Ed and Marco decide Tribe is about as thrilling as . . . chess club.' (I quite like chess but it's not a good thing to admit.)

'Wicked,' said Fifty.

'Do you think it will work?' said Bee. She was smiling already. I could see she thought it was a winner

'Yes, I do,' said Fifty. 'We didn't manage to scare him off, so we'll bore him to death. You can tell him about every goal you've ever scored, Copper Pie.'

TRIBERS' MOST BORING TOPICS

COPPER PIE: Football, football, football, football, football, football, football . . .

KEENER: Reciting the number plates of every car any member of his family or friends has ever owned.

BEE: Her lecture about all the things people do every day that damage the planet.

JONNO: Insects, arachnids (spiders to the rest of us), moths, butterflies.

FIFTY: Probably Rose.

'OK. We've got a plan. You ask them to come, Jonno,' said Bee. 'Marco likes you.'

Jonno strolled off, hands in his pockets, hair bobbing up and down.

welcoming
Marco and Ed

Doodle was waiting at the school gates. He's not getting any better behaved, even though he's been puppy trained. He jumps up at everyone. We all avoid him. Jonno is Doodle's only real friend.

'Hello, you lovely dog.' Jonno ruffled Doodle's fur and Doodle snapped at his fingers. Jonno did the whole turning away thing again. It's meant to teach the dog what's good and what isn't. Jonno's been trying to help Bee, but Bee's mum keeps ruining everything.

'Mum, I don't need an escort home from school *every* day,' said Bee.

'Don't you want to see Doodle? He misses you.'

Bee rolled her eyes. 'Mum, he's a dog. He doesn't miss me. He only misses food.'

Bee's mum looked shocked, so Bee quickly gave Doodle a couple of pats. 'Come on, then. See you later, Tribers.'

BEE'S PUPPY TRAINING TIPS

Start as soon as you get the dog. Don't be all soft and let it jump up at you, snap, and sleep in your bed, because when the puppy gets bigger, jumping up means knocking over, snapping means you lose some fingers and your bed becomes the dog's.

Dogs are pack animals. You are part of the pack. Make sure you're the leader and be fair and consistent. (This also works with children.) Dogs and kids don't understand what they're meant to do if one day you're nice, and the next day you're not.

The best way to have a nice dog that people like is to reward it when it does something good. This works better than punishing it when it's bad. (This is also true of children.)

If your puppy chews your mum's party shoe, don't let it see you laugh. Dogs understand more than you think.

'I'll come with you,' said Jonno. 'Bye.'

Me, Fifty and Copper Pie went down the alley on our own. Fifty said we could all pretend to be so boring we sent ourselves to sleep and him and Copper Pie laughed about that nearly all the way home. After they both turned off, I walked really slowly to mine, thinking about Tribe. We were five, like the *Famous Five* books that my dad's always going on about. But I was worried we were going to end up as six.

I wanted to believe in Jonno's idea, but it was difficult to think of Tribe as boring when it's actually the best thing *ever*. I gave up and decided that if I could kick the same stone all the way home the problem would go away.

(My stone went under a bus and didn't come back out.)

I bolted down tea (gammon and my second jacket potato of the day) because I wanted to be there at the start of the meeting. I don't know why. Maybe it was because I wanted to get there before Marco and Ed, to show I was a real Triber – a founder.

'Slow down, darling, or you'll choke,' said Mum.

'And shut your mouth when you chew,' said Flo, the world's most irritating little sister. (And to think I nearly liked her for a while after the Fat Cat business.)

I opened my mouth wide to show her the contents. Mum slapped me on the back and I nearly did choke. After I'd managed to demolish my dinner I scraped the plate with my knife ('Keener! Don't do that,' shouted Amy) and got up to go.

'I'm off. Meeting at the Tribehouse.'

'I heard Marco tell Ed he was going to the Tribehouse

too,' said Flo. *How does a Year 3 know everything that goes on?*

'So what?' I said.

Flo made a horrible face. 'Soooo . . . Marco isn't a Triber.'

'But he's a friend,' I said, even though he isn't really.

'That's nice. Since when?' said Mum.

'Since we went surfing on Sunday,' I said.

'And now it's Wednesday,' said Amy. 'And on Monday you were ill in bed. What's so great about Marco that he gets to go to the Tribe shack after two days?'

I left, but Amy's words swam around in my head, like sharks.

I scrambled through the cat flap and was first in. I opened the safe and took out the subs to count our money while I was waiting. I fished in the back and pulled out the fact sheets and the scroll. Fifty came in and took his usual seat, on the safe.

'What's all that for?' he asked.

'To show Marco what it's all about. If he thinks it's like homework that might put him off.'

We sat and waited for the others.

There was a noise outside. It was Bee, tying Doodle to the leg of Fifty's outside table.

'What's Doodle doing here?' said Fifty.

'Mum was going out and she didn't want Doodle to be lonely so I've got to look after him.'

'What about your dad?' said Fifty.

'Well, he was happy for a bit when the boys moved out but now he says that Doodle takes up as much room as the boys did so he refuses to have anything to so with him.'

'He's not going to move out again, is he?' said Fifty.

'No. Mum said if he ever did anything like that again she'd change the locks. And she meant it.'

Bee came inside. Terrible whining started and got louder.

'Maybe your dad will grow to like him?' I said, although it didn't seem likely.

'He says he'd rather have the twins back.'

The whining was unbearable, like a baby being tortured. Bee stayed where she was.

'Aren't you going to . . . cuddle him?' said Fifty.

Copper Pie came in at that moment and snorted. 'Wuss. It's a dog. They're for chasing sticks, not snogging.'

'And what are baby elephants for?' said Fifty. 'Are they for snogging?' And then he whispered, 'Trumpet. Trumpet.'

Copper Pie went mad, chasing Fifty round the hut. It's better not to mention Copper Pie's cuddly elephant, aka Trumpet.

'At least I didn't wear my Thomas the Tank 'jamas to school under my clothes,' said Copper Pie.

We've all got secrets that aren't secret, if you get what I mean. I looked at my three old friends, Bee, Copper Pie and Fifty and the thoughts, like sharks, that had been swimming around ever since I left home finally took a bite. Amy was so right (I never thought I'd hear myself think that!). Marco was a good, some would say excellent, surfer. He was cool. So what! That didn't make him a Triber. That didn't mean he would agree with what we do, believe in what we believe in, be a loyal friend. We were a Tribe of five, not six, and I was about to be *so* boring, no one would want to be a Triber!

'Hey Doodle.' Jonno was in the garden. Marco and Ed were bound to be with him. I was ready.

'P904KPG. S5TMA. KY02NVQ. ML57BOY . . .'

'Hello,' said Jonno.

'Hi,' said Ed.

Marco was behind them. He had his board resting on the top of his skate shoe.

'JAY616D. T48AWL.'

'What's he doing?' said Ed, meaning me.

'He's trying to remember every number plate anyone he knows has ever had. He does it every meeting,' said Fifty.

It was hard not to smile, but I wasn't going to crack. There was too much at stake. 'E649PUG. KY54DTB . . .'

'So, what do we do then?' said Ed.

'When Keener's finished we usually let Copper Pie give a match report from his football game on Saturday.' Fifty's face was brilliant. Deadly serious.

'OK,' said Ed. 'But you go surfing too, don't you? You don't just stay in here.' He looked around.

'That was a good day,' said Fifty. Marco nodded. 'We might do it again next summer.'

'Next summer? Don't you mean next week?' said Ed. Marco started tapping his board. It was quite annoying but I didn't falter.

'BR09FGX. Y717GGS . . .'

'We've got too much paperwork to do to have another day out.' Fifty pointed at the fact files I'd got out of the safe.

No one said anything after that, except me. I carried on with my number plates. 'CL58HSE . . .'

'Not long now, Ed,' said Fifty.

I wasn't sure how long I could go on. Surely they wouldn't believe the Tribers did this every Wednesday? Thankfully Jonno spoke up. 'It's not usually this boring. Sometimes we play board games. We could play one now if you like?'

'We might go to the park,' said Ed. 'What do you think, Marco?'

Ed was already out of the door. I saw him flick his board up with his toe and catch it. Marco followed him out.

'Have a nice meeting. I go with Ed. Thanks for ask me.' He waved.

I checked out my fellow Tribers. Copper Pie made a fist and punched the air. We waited until the voices faded completely.

'Mission accomplished,' I said.

'You were like a robot,' said Fifty.

'Well, that's over,' said Bee. 'And I'm so glad. We don't know anything about Marco. He'll be happier with Ed.'

'We don't know if he wears Thomas the Tank 'jamas,' said Copper Pie.

'We don't know if he has a favourite cuddly elephant,' said Fifty.

I joined in. 'And we don't know if he walks in his sleep.'

Bee gave me her best mean look – we all know she goes walkabout and talkabout in the night – and got me straight back. 'And we don't know if he goes strawberry colour every time he's asked a question in class.'

Unfair, I thought.

We all looked pretty pleased. The only one who didn't was Jonno.

'What's up, Jonno?' said Fifty. 'Did you want to go with them?'

'It's not that,' said Jonno.

'What is it then?' said Bee.

He sighed. 'I'm a Triber, but not as much as you lot are. I'm the odd one out. I'm still the stranger.'

I didn't know what he was on about – there's nothing strange about Jonno, except his hair – but Bee did. 'The fact that we've all known each other since Keener was in nappies' (I was *not* in nappies at pre-school) 'doesn't mean we're better Tribers.'

'It does.'

'No, it doesn't. And anyway, we're waiting to find out your most embarrassing moment and then we're going to tease you *forever*, Frizzy.'

Chicken Piri-Piri

That was the nickname, Sass, the girl in the alley, called Jonno. And it gave me an idea. I reeled off every bit of information I knew about Jonno, from the layout of his room and all the stuff in it, to the things he'd done since he met us, and I threw in the date of his birthday (because I remember numbers) and everything else he'd told us about his life, like the fact that he used to hold the label in his school shorts.

When I'd finished there were smiles all round. And Jonno's was the biggest. 'Put it there,' I said.

I slapped down my hand and they all piled theirs on top for the Tribe handshake. ONE, TWO, THREE. They flew in the air.

Tribe had had a rocky couple of weeks, nearly losing Copper Pie and then nearly gaining Marco. It was like a test, and we'd passed. No one can leave, and no one can join. That's what we decided at the beginning. We had to stay true to what Tribe was all about. We knew that now. And it felt good. It didn't mean Ed and Marco couldn't be our friends – in fact I'd already suggested another surf trip with Marco. But they couldn't be Tribers.

The whining started again. We all looked over at Bee.

'Do I have to?' she asked.

We nodded. So she got up and we followed.

'Sit,' she said. And Doodle sat. 'Good dog.' She gave him something from a bag strapped to the loop on her jeans. He gobbled it up.

'They're the treats,' said Jonno. 'It's how you train puppies, by rewarding them when they're good.'

Bee stroked Doodle's back and for once he didn't snap at her. I think she was surprised. 'Shall I take you home?' she asked.

I know dogs can't speak English but I think Doodle understood.

'Come on then.' Bee undid his lead and he stood by her side waiting for her to walk off.

'You're a natural,' said Jonno.

She peeked back at us over her shoulder. 'Why wouldn't I be?'

'And you've got a big head,' said Copper Pie.

Bee left with Doodle. Jonno left with Copper Pie. Fifty went up to the house to read Probably Rose her bedtime story through the bars of her cot. As I walked home from the Tribehouse I wondered whether we would be Tribers forever. That's what Bee said to Jonno – that we'd tease him forever. I liked that idea. That whatever happened, we'd always be Tribe.

The Tribers will soon return in a new book,
so here's a sneak peek at the next *Tribe* story!

Keener
Bunks Off

late
for lunch

It was sausages for school lunch – result! I turned round to start off a Tribe handshake (only really meant for great triumphs) but after I slapped down my hand, only three others followed. There should have been four. I stopped my second hand in mid-flight.

'Where's Copper Pie?'

Bee's head, Fifty's head and Jonno's head all turned to look behind. There was Alice, and behind her Marco and Ed. But no Copper Pie.

'He must be here. He's not exactly going to miss lunch, is he?' said Bee.

'Same,' said Fifty.

They were right. Copper Pie never skips a meal. In fact he has extra snacks in between to ensure his stomach is never less than half full.

'Maybe he snuck in early,' said Jonno.

On Tuesdays we have to wait until last to go in for dinner. It's a killer. I scanned the tables to see if our redheaded friend was already munching . . . No.

The thump took me by surprise. It was right in the middle of my back. I lurched forwards and nearly crushed a Year 3 (easily done).

'Sorry,' I said, before turning round to face my out-of-breath friend, 'What did you do that for?'

'Sorry, Keener. Couldn't stop in time,' said Copper Pie. 'I smelt the sausages.' (Pant. Pant.) 'Didn't want to miss out.'

'Where were you?' said Fifty.

Copper Pie didn't answer, because someone else did.

'He was somewhere he shouldn't have been,' said Callum, enemy of Tribe, enemy of all decent humans. He walked towards us with a knowing look on his face.

'Go away, Hog,' said Copper Pie.

'Why? Got something to hide?' said Callum.

'No,' said Copper Pie. He stepped so close to Callum, he was nearly treading on the toes of his trainers. 'I just don't like you.'

It looked like trouble, but thankfully Alice - the most irritating girl in the class, except on this one occasion - decided to get involved.

'You've jumped the queue, Callum. Get to the back or I'll tell . . .' She looked around for a teacher. 'I'll tell Mr Morris.'

'Go ahead. I'll tell him Copper Pie pushed in too, and we

can carry on with our little chat at the back, on our own.'
Callum was definitely up for a fight.

'You're wrong there,' said Bee. 'Copper Pie was here all the
time. Wasn't he, Tribers?'

There was general nodding. I don't really like lying but . . .

Callum looked at Alice. Behind her, I could see Mr Morris
walking our way. 'You'll back me up, won't you Alice?' he said.

She stared straight back at him . . . and shook her head.

Go Alice! She's not a Triber (and never could be), but I
decided to try to be a bit nicer to her.

Callum curled his lip, like a villain in an old film, said, 'I'll
be watching you,' and disappeared to the back of the line.

'What was that all about?' asked Jonno.

We all looked at Copper Pie.

'Is it all right if I get my sausages first?' he said.

When we'd all got our food, we sat at our favourite table
in the corner.

'Go on then, spill the beans,' said Bee.

'I think Callum saw me coming through the gates.'

No big deal, I thought. Copper Pie must have wellied the
ball right out of the school grounds. It happens regularly.

'He won't tell on you,' said Bee. 'It's not worth it.'

'Same,' said Fifty.

'Depends how much he saw,' said Copper Pie.

Jonno laughed. 'Why? Did you do a quick raid on the café
while you were there? Did you steal a hot chocolate?'

I laughed too. But Copper Pie stayed deadly serious.

'What is it?' said Bee, flicking her black fringe out of her eyes to give him her best stare.

'Callum was outside the gates too, getting his ball.' Copper Pie paused.

'And?' said Bee.

'And he might have seen me coming from the alley.' Copper Pie winced.

It was very confusing. Why would Copper Pie be coming out of the alley when he should have been in the playground? I hadn't seen him, but I assumed he'd been practising in the goal. He often does.

'But where had you been?' said Fifty.

'I bunked off,' said Copper Pie. (I gasped. This was bad.) 'There was something I had to do. And the trouble is, I've got to do it again tomorrow, and the next day . . .'

I had no idea what the 'something' was but I could see what was coming. It was going to be another problem for Tribe to sort out. Why we couldn't have a few normal days being normal children, I didn't know. But one of the Tribers was in a fix, and that meant we were all in a fix. I waited, with a bit of a worry growing inside, to hear the details.

What is Copper Pie up to?
Find out in *Tribe: Keener Bunks Off*
978 1 84812 093 8
Coming Soon